ALSO BY CAROL HUGHES

Dirty Magic
Jack Black and the Ship of Thieves

The PRINCESS
and the
UNICORN

The *PRINCESS*
and the
UNICORN

Carol Hughes

Random House 🏠 New York

Text copyright © 2009 by Carol Hughes
Jacket art copyright © 2009 by Juliana Kolesova
Jacket design by Michelle Gengaro-Kokmen

Published in the United States by Random House Children's Books,
a division of Random House, Inc., New York.

Random House and colophon are registered trademarks of Random House, Inc.

Visit us on the Web! www.randomhouse.com/kids

Educators and librarians, for a variety of teaching tools,
visit us at www.randomhouse.com/teachers

Library of Congress Cataloging-in-Publication Data
Hughes, Carol.
The princess and the unicorn / by Carol Hughes. — 1st ed.
p. cm.
Summary: Joyce the fairy has the adventure she has always dreamed of when she joins
forces with a human princess to rescue the unicorn stolen from Swinley Forest,
placing the forest and its fairy community in grave danger.
ISBN 978-0-375-85562-7 (trade) — ISBN 978-0-375-95562-4 (lib. bdg.) —
ISBN 978-0-375-85563-4 (pbk.)
[1. Fairies—Fiction. 2. Princesses—Fiction. 3. Unicorns—Fiction. 4. Adventure and
adventurers—Fiction. 5. Forests and forestry—Fiction. 6. England—Fiction.] I. Title.
PZ7.H873116Pri 2009
[Fic]—dc22
2008003034

Printed in the United States of America
10 9 8 7 6 5 4 3 2 1
First Edition

To John, Faith, and Shane

CONTENTS

The PRINCESS
and the
UNICORN

Chapter 1

The Fairy

Swinley Castle, that world-famous ancient monument and official Royal residence, stands atop a high hill some thirty miles west of London. It is one of the most splendid castles in the world, and on a clear day the magnificent honey-colored turrets and towers can be seen from miles away.

Like many Royal buildings nowadays, Swinley Castle is open to tourists for a small entrance fee. A visitor may view the great staterooms, the chapel, and the Royal kitchens. They may even see a Royal bedchamber or two, but no more. The remainder of the castle is strictly out of bounds. This is because it is still used frequently by the Royal Family. The king, the queen, and their only child, H.R.H. the Princess Eleanor, often occupy a wing of private rooms.

When the Royal Family is in residence, the union flag flies from the castle's flagpole. But don't think that if you are visiting the castle and the flag is flying, you will catch sight of any of Their Highnesses. They tend to keep to their own quarters when the castle is open to the public, and who could blame them? They may be Royal, but they are still people.

Like the castle itself, the extensive grounds of Swinley are beautiful. Within the castle wall there are the Royal gardens—kitchen, herb, and formal—and a few velvety green lawns where the princess occasionally plays croquet with her governess. Beyond the castle wall a large meadow rolls away to the south. It dips down into a valley and then rises in a long sweep to the edge of the Great Forest of Swinley, one of the last truly ancient forests in Europe.

Swinley Forest is fiercely protected. No human, neither gardener nor tree surgeon nor member of the Royal Family, has set foot in those woods for a century. The forest is an ecological miracle and a national treasure. It is also a little bit spooky.

One summer morning when Their Majesties were

still slumbering in their Royal beds, much was happening in a part of their kingdom that none of them knew existed.

The ancient fairy town of Swinley Hope is situated in the exact center of the ancient forest of Swinley, and it is here, in this long-forgotten outpost of the fairy world, that our story begins.

It was market day in Swinley Hope, and although the sun was only just up, carts laden with all sorts of summer goodies were rolling into the market square. Merchants and farmers were setting up their stalls. Wild strawberries as big as a fairy's head, bushels of tiny truffles, and mounds of early cranberries were being carefully arranged on the wooden tables.

It promised to be a pleasant day. Nearly all the fairies, elves, and pixies who lived in the vast expanse of Swinley Forest came to town on market day. They came to sell, to buy, to gossip, or to just enjoy themselves.

High above the square a young fairy by the name of Joyce lay on her belly along a twig at the top of her home tree. Although she'd been up for hours, she was still in her pajamas and her hair was mussed from sleep.

"Ah, summer," she said, sitting up and stretching

out her wings behind her. "Summer is absolutely my favorite season." And she really meant it. Then she remembered that every season was her favorite season, and she laughed, causing the twig to bounce beneath her weight.

Joyce and her family lived, like the other fairies in Swinley Hope, in a house that was built into the trunk of one of the trees. Joyce's house was the last house at the top of a horse chestnut tree that stood along the southern edge of the square.

Being so high up on the tree meant that theirs was not a large house. In fact, Joyce could stand in the kitchen/living/dining room and, by stretching out her arms, easily touch both walls at once. When she and her two sisters and her parents were all in that room together there was barely space to stand, and if her sisters decided to preen their wings at the same time, there was no room whatsoever. Joyce loved their small house, though. Living in the last house on the trunk meant she could climb out and sit in the branches and no one would wander past her on their way home. It was, in her opinion, a delightful place to live.

Joyce hugged her knees to her chest and smiled. In a couple of weeks the school term would be over and she'd be able to spend her days paddling in the brook, or collecting elderflower petals, or even, perhaps, trekking in the forest, where she could spend a quiet hour or two staring into the trees beyond. Who knew, perhaps she'd catch a glimpse of the unicorn. Just the thought of it made Joyce tingle with excitement.

She sighed happily and tilted her face upward. As always in the summer months, the sky was barely visible through the thick canopy of bright leaves. Only small, irregular pieces of it could be seen between the jagged green edges. The sky looked so small from where she sat, but she knew that up there beyond the leaves, the sky was vast and limitless. How high, she wondered, could a fairy fly, if she flew straight up as fast as she could?

But even the fairies who were still young enough to fly were never allowed to fly above the treetops. It was too dangerous. Joyce clearly remembered the day her kindergarten teacher had warned her about it. Most of her classmates had just nodded and accepted what the teacher said without question, but not Joyce. Joyce had always been full of questions.

"Why not, Miss Bracket?" she'd piped up. "Why can't we fly up there?"

Miss Bracket had smiled at her indulgently.

"Because, Joyce, it's very dangerous. The hot sun would frazzle a fairy to nothing in less than a second."

Joyce's hand had instantly shot up again. "What if

it's a rainy day?" she'd asked. "Could you fly up there then?"

Miss Bracket's smile had faded. "No, Joyce. Don't you remember? Wet wings do not work."

"What if it's a cloudy day?" Joyce had persisted.

"No, Joyce," Miss Bracket had replied with a weary sigh. "On cloudy days the wind would snatch you up and blow you into the vast empty sky. Then you'd be lost forever, and how do you think your parents would feel about that?"

Joyce had still had questions. "What if there was no wind that day?" she'd wanted to ask, but the exasperated look on Miss Bracket's face had warned her to keep quiet.

Joyce had never dared to fly up past the top leaves of the trees. She had never broken that rule, but you could say that she had bent it slightly. On fine, moonless nights she had often flown to the top of her tree and sat just beneath the upper layer of leaves so that she could gaze out at the stars. First she would find Polaris, the North Star, then she would search for the constellations, the Great Bear and the Little Dipper and, harder to see, Draco the Dragon.

She turned her head slightly and stared at the leaves around her, marveling as always that no matter how hard she searched she never found two that were exactly the same. This fascinated her because when you looked at a whole tree, the leaves seemed to be exactly alike, but when you looked carefully at them, they were just as different from each other as one fairy is from the next. The color might be a shade lighter or the veins more wiggly or the serrations along the edge deeper or more irregular.

"Joyce! JOYCE!" her mother called. "Are you going to school today or not?"

"Coming!" Joyce cried as she scrambled to her feet. She didn't want to be late for school. She hurried along the branch and squeezed in through the window of her sleeping nook. She was out of her pajamas and into her school uniform in a flash. She wriggled her wings through the elasticized holes in the back of her blouse and jammed her feet into her shoes. She gave her hair a quick brush, tried to do something about her wings, then darted through the door.

In the cramped kitchen/dining/living room, Joyce's mom and her twin sisters, Star (short for Star-Lily) and Chryssie (short for Chrysanthemum), were sitting at the small table finishing their breakfast when Joyce clattered down the stairs and burst in amongst them.

"Well, good *afternoon!*" said her mother. "I thought the Bigguns must have come and snatched you in the night."

Joyce glanced at her sisters and caught them exchanging the here-we-go-again look they always exchanged whenever their mother mentioned Bigguns. No one in the forest believed in Bigguns, or big people, anymore—no one except their mom and a few other extremely superstitious fairies.

It was embarrassing. Their mom was convinced that Bigguns had once, long ago, come tramping through the forest to snatch fairies from their beds and carry them away in cages.

Joyce may not have believed in Bigguns, but she loved all the stories, especially the ones Sam the street sweeper told. His tales were full of fascinating details—for example, in his stories most big people didn't believe in fairies. Which was funny, especially as most fairies in Swinley Hope didn't believe in Bigguns.

"I know you three think I'm batty," said Joyce's mom as she set more toast on the table. "But I'm not ashamed to say I believe in them—have done all my life. Mind, it's not something I want to be proved right about. I may believe in them, but I never want to see one." Their mom shuddered at the thought. The twins rolled their eyes.

Joyce flumped down beside Chrysanthemum and grabbed a piece of toast.

"Joy-hoi-ce! Watch out," griped Chryssie, scooting out of the way so that Joyce didn't crush her perfectly folded wings. She twisted around, trying to see what damage had been done. Star checked her sister's wings.

"It's okay, Chryss," said Star. "Joyce didn't get you. They still look fabulous. Come on, let's go before she splatters food on us."

Joyce stuck her tongue out at her sisters and threatened them with the greasy butter knife. The twins shrieked and hurried through the door. "Bye, Mom!" they called as they ran down the stairs outside.

"Here's your lunch, Joyce." Her mom set two neatly wrapped sandwiches on the table. "The other one's for Sam, if you see him. I daresay he'd appreciate it."

"Thanks, Mom." Joyce had nearly finished her breakfast when her father walked through the door.

"Hi, Dad," she said cheerfully through a mouthful of toast.

"Eat, don't speak," said her mom. "You'll be late."

"Morning," said her dad, winking at her and sitting down. Joyce smiled back. He looked exhausted.

Market days were always the busiest for him because part of his job as a forester was to make certain that none of the produce for sale had been taken from any unauthorized areas of the forest. As the guardians of the great forest, the fairies of Swinley Hope worked tirelessly to make certain that the natural cycle of the forest was not disturbed or disrupted by anything, including the fairies themselves. To this end, the Alder Fairies kept a strict eye on which trees, plants, shrubs, and bushes could be harvested for food in any given season. They made sure that berries and other fruits were taken only once every three or four seasons from any particular plant.

Every market day Joyce's dad had to rise well before dawn and stand on the dusty road, checking each cart's load as it came into town. Joyce knew that after he'd finished his breakfast he would still have a full day of his usual forestry work to do. This month he was on dell duty, which meant that every day he had to walk many fairy miles through the forest to a dell full of bluebells. Once there, he carefully checked over the petals, leaves, and stalks in that day's measured section. Then, after he had made absolutely sure that all was well and had fixed any problems he'd found and had made a full report in his notebook, he walked all the way home. The next day he would be off again on his long journey through the forest.

Joyce knew her dad loved his work. She knew it by the way his face lit up at supper when he told them about his day. Joyce liked to hear how he ate his lunch sitting beneath the towering purply-blue bell-shaped flowers. When the school term was over, she hoped he'd let her go with him like he had last summer. It would be nice to have their lunch together in the dell before the bluebells were gone.

"Joyce!" said her mother. "You were off in a dream as usual. Come on, poppet, school! Remember it's market day."

Joyce finished her toast, grabbed her bag, and was about to hurry out the door when her mother caught her.

"Hold on," she said as she started to fix Joyce's wings. School rules required wings to be neatly folded for class.

"Ow, Mo-hom!" Joyce squirmed as her mother tried to make the unruly wings lay flat.

"They'll have to do," said her mother, not at all pleased with the result. "Off you go."

Joyce quickly downed the rest of her sloeberry juice, grabbed a second piece of toast to eat on the way, kissed her dad on the forehead, and rushed out the door. A second later she popped her head back in. "Dad, can I come with you to the bluebel—?"

"Joyce! GO!" cried her mother, throwing a tea towel at the door in exasperation.

Chapter 2

THE PRINCESS

While Joyce had been sitting on the tree branch outside her window, gazing at the market below, less than half a mile away in human terms, ten-year-old big person Princess Eleanor Charlotte Anya Ilona Grace Victoria (known affectionately by her governess as Princess Baby), Heiress Presumptive to the English throne, beloved and only child of Their Majesties the king and queen, was lying sound asleep in the magnificent four-poster bed in her Royal bedchamber. Her pink-pajamed legs had kicked off the heavy covers, and her long blond curls, which had been tightly braided by her governess before bed to keep them from getting knotty in the night, now ranged messily over her 1,000-thread-count Egyptian cotton pillowcases.

All was silent in the princess's bedchamber, and it would have been completely dark but for a single sliver of sunlight squeaking between the velvet drapes and piercing the gloom. As the sun rose higher, this shaft of light lengthened and crept across the bedroom floor. Slowly, it crossed the expanse of pink carpet and climbed up the ornately carved bedstead. It vanished at the top, reappearing moments later on the embroidered quilt that lay scrambled on the bed. The light inched its way up the covers and over the quilts and then, when it reached the multitude of satin pillows arranged at the head of the bed, it shone directly onto the sleeping princess's left eyelid.

The princess groaned, turned away from the light, and buried her face in the cushions. She was not a morning person.

The door to the princess's bedroom opened quietly and a small, thin woman entered. This was Ms. Margaret Merrieweather, governess, assistant, and companion to Her Royal Highness.

"Princess Baby?" she called in a high, sweet voice. When no response came, she pursed her lips, smoothed the front of her neat black dress, and, straightening the single strand of pearls at her neck, approached the princess's bed.

"Come along, Princess Baby, time to get up. Wakey wakey, egg and bakey!" Ms. Merrieweather trilled, gently shaking the apparently sleeping princess with a thin white hand.

"Five more minutes, please, Merrie," begged the princess, pulling the covers over her head.

The governess laughed her charming, tinkling laugh, took hold of the silk covers, and yanked them off the bed. The princess remained curled on the mattress with her eyes closed. The governess humphed, then turned and strode across the room.

"Come along now, Princess Baby!" she bellowed. "Surely you don't want to stay in bed on such a lovely—" Merrie arrived at the window and took hold of the drapes.

"No . . . Merrie . . . please—don't," pleaded the princess, sitting up.

"—SUNNY—"

"Merrie—"

"—DAY!" Merrie flung open the curtains. Bright morning sunlight flooded the room.

Merrie turned triumphantly, her skinny form silhouetted against the light. "Good, you're awake. I'll draw your bath," she said as she disappeared into the bathroom and turned on the taps full blast. The princess slid off her bed and watched clouds of steam billow out of the bathroom. What, she wondered, was the point of being a princess if you never got to sleep late? Perhaps she should demand it. She shook her head. Merrie would never let her get away with that.

The governess emerged from the steam and trotted to the bed. She set her hands on the princess's shoulders and, with a firm push, steered her toward the bathroom.

"Merrie, why do we always have to start lessons so ear—" she had started to say when she was interrupted by the sound of dogs barking outside. "Oh!" the princess gasped. Wriggling free of Merrie's hands, she dashed to the window.

"Merrie!" she cried. "Is the hunt today?" The princess laid her face sideways against the glass, trying to see into the courtyard. "I thought it was tomorrow. But it's definitely today. Look! There's the Master of the Hounds." The princess spun around. Her eyes were bright with excitement. "This is great news. We'll have such a super time, you'll see!" She stopped when she saw the governess's face. "Merrie. You don't have to come, if you don't want to. I know how you feel about horses."

Merrie gave a nervous laugh and crossed to the

princess's dressing table. "Ah, ha ha. No, no, my dear," she protested. She looked at herself in the mirror, pursed her lips, turned her head this way and that, and patted her tight coppery curls. She caught the princess's eye and smiled. "No, my dear, I promised I would ride. And you know how I never like to break a promise."

"Captain Simperington will look after me."

Merrie picked up a hairbrush and laughed again. "No, I'd feel I was failing in my duties if I didn't come." She leaned toward the mirror and frowned at her chin. Three black bristles poked through the powder. No matter how often she plucked them, they always grew back. She turned to face the princess. "Besides," she said brightly, "I *want* to hunt. *Really.* I do."

The princess's face lit up. "Oh, Merrie!" She grinned. "I am so glad. Didn't I always say I'd make a horsewoman of you? Hunting is so much fun! You're going to love it!" Princess Eleanor darted into the bathroom, singing, "A-hunting we will go, a-hunting we will go!" at the top of her voice.

When her Royal charge had vanished into the steamy bathroom, Margaret Merrieweather stood and twisted the hairbrush in her hands. Her mouth twitched and a vein in her temple pulsated. Merrie hated horses.

A phone began to ring. Merrie quickly pulled an ultra-slim purple cell phone from her pocket and, after scowling at the caller's number, pressed a key to send the call to voice mail. After a quick glance at the bathroom door, she jabbed rapidly at the keys, thumbs flying over the numbers as she composed a message. She smiled as she hit send.

"I didn't know you got a new phone!" Merrie's head shot up. The princess was standing at the bathroom door, wrapped in a fluffy pink towel. "I like the color. Can I see it?" she asked.

"Only if you want to be late for the hunt, my precious," replied Merrie, slipping the phone back into her pocket and nodding at the clock.

"Oh!" cried Eleanor. "Can I wear my new jodhpurs?"

Merrie smiled indulgently. "Of course. Let me get them for you, Your Highness." She hurried to the princess's walk-in wardrobe and disappeared inside.

Chapter 3

The Unicorn

Joyce trotted down the steps that spiraled around the trunk of her home tree, glancing every so often over the bark balustrade to check how crowded the market had become. The school was only on the far side of the clearing, and on nonmarket days Joyce was able to run all the way and arrive before the bell rang. But on market days there were too many stalls and carts and fairies in her way. Today it was packed. Joyce stopped and stared at the throng.

A few of the Alder Fairies in their bright emerald caps stood in front of the town hall, a beautiful building housed in the base of the oldest oak tree in the town.

"Joyce!" Joyce turned and saw her mother behind her on the steps. She was carrying a basket on her arm. Joyce moved out of the way to let her pass.

"Goodness me," her mother said. "I didn't expect to catch up with you. You should be long gone by now. I'll see you later. Must dash—I want to get the shopping done before I go to work. Bye!"

Joyce tried to keep up with her mom, but the stair rises were uneven, and she found it difficult to hurry without stumbling. She watched her mother nimbly scampering down the steps with her beautifully folded wings bouncing prettily on her back. Joyce's own wings had not stayed folded. They never did. They flapped about messily and kept catching on the bark.

Joyce looked across the market. She could see the younger fairies from her school whizzing over the crowds. It wasn't fair. She could be at school in less than a minute if she flew, but she didn't dare. Her mother would be mortified, her father would be disappointed, her sisters would be furious, and she would never hear the end of it. How many times did she have to be told: the respectable fairies of Swinley Forest simply *do not fly.*

It wasn't that the respectable fairies didn't have wings. They did. They all had good-sized gossamer wings that glinted a vibrant bluish-green in the light. It wasn't that they didn't know how to fly. Without exception they had all flown as youngsters. Flying when young was encouraged because it ensured that wings grew long and straight. But when fairies reached the age of ten or so, their parents, their teachers, and even their peers persuaded them to give it up. Why?

Because flying was *common*. It was unseemly. It was uncouth. And no decent, self-respecting fairy would be caught dead flapping his or her beautiful wings and actually *flying*. The very idea. No. Birds flew. Insects flew. The odd rough, ill-bred fairy might thumb their nose at convention and fly. Respectable fairies most certainly did not.

The strangest thing was that these same respectable fairies were extremely proud of their wings and took exceptionally good care of them. They loved to preen them, washing each wing over and over till the colors shone. Hours were spent folding the wings into intricate, elegant styles—styles involving complicated, secret wing-folding techniques that had been handed down from mother to daughter, father to son. The folded wings were then trailed down the fairy's back and sometimes decorated with ribbons and petals. For this elaborate and desirable wing folding to be possible, it was important that the wing muscles were kept soft and pliant. The flimsier the gossamer, the more pliable the wings, and the more pliable they were, the flatter they lay. The longest, softest, weakest wings were considered the most beautiful and very much admired.

Here was another mark against flying. Flying ruined a fairy's wings. If a fairy flew every day, his or her soft gossamer wings would become misshapen and muscular. Muscular wings could not be neatly folded. Muscular wings were not elegant. Muscular wings were ugly and coarse. By flying after the age of ten, when the wings were fully formed but not yet "ruined," a fairy ran the risk of being burdened with leathery wings for the rest of his or her life. Naturally, every well-meaning parent did their best to prevent this, and Joyce's mother and father were no exception.

Since she'd turned ten, almost a year ago, Joyce had tried to give up flying but hadn't managed it yet. She couldn't bear the idea of never flying again.

When she reached the bottom of the tree, Joyce could see it would take her forever to get through the market. She was definitely going to be late, unless . . . she flew!

"Everyone is at the market," she reasoned. "No one will see me." She'd have to fly around the town and that was much farther, but at least she'd be on time. She turned and began to run. When she reached the edge of town she shook out her wings and took off into the trees.

Joyce sped through the air. She was an excellent flyer, which was another reason that it had been so hard to give it up. She loved the feeling of swerving and slicing through the forest with her wings droning behind her. When she reached the elm with two trunks, she shifted her weight and veered south.

She was almost at school. She just had to take one more turn, cross over the brook that ran beside the town, land out of sight somewhere, and run the rest of the way to the gate. She might even arrive early.

She was just flying over the brook when something deep in the forest caught her eye. A flash of gold. At first she thought it was the glitter of sunlight on the water upstream. But there was something unusual about it. It flashed again. Joyce stared at it, trying to puzzle it out. She would have been far better off looking where she was going.

SLAM! Joyce hit a pine tree with a colossal bang and dropped to the ground. Luckily she hadn't been flying too high, and a thick covering of needles on the ground cushioned her landing.

She stood up shakily and, as she did so, saw the light again. She shielded her eyes and peered upstream. All of a sudden she knew what she was looking at. It was the unicorn of Swinley Forest, and he was close—fifty fairy yards away, perhaps less.

He was drinking from the sparkling brook. Ripples of light bounced off the water and danced over his pure white coat. His horn, a golden spiral, gleamed against the milky white of his forehead, and his hooves, one of which he held aloft as he drank, were the same polished gold as his horn. His long, straight mane and tail were a paler gold, and strands of them sparkled as they caught the light.

Joyce could barely believe her luck. Hardly anyone had ever seen the unicorn. Forester fairies on rare occasions had caught a glimpse of him, but it was usually only a distant sighting, a flicker of gold in the depths of the trees. It was really only the fact that the forest was thriving that told them the unicorn was still within the woods at all. Not that the fairies thought he would ever leave—at least they hoped he wouldn't. That, they knew, would be disastrous. If the unicorn ever left, it wouldn't matter how hard the fairies worked. No forest could survive for long without its unicorn.

Joyce stared until every last detail of his beauty was engraved on her mind—the softness of his muzzle, the darkness of his eyes, the exact shape of his forelock as it curled around the base of the horn and fell forward between his beautiful eyes.

DANG! DANG! DANG! Joyce jumped. It was the school bell. The unicorn's head shot up. For a moment the fairy and the unicorn stared at each other, then the unicorn flared his nostrils, tossed his head, and galloped off into the woods.

DANG! DANG! DANG!

Joyce had to go. There'd be no time to run the last part. She'd have to fly all the way to the school door, but she didn't care if she was spotted flying. She couldn't stop grinning. She had seen the unicorn! She took to the air and, turning right, sped up the street to school. She couldn't wait to tell someone.

Halfway up the street she saw a solitary figure walking broom in hand toward the town. His shock of white hair made him immediately recognizable.

"Sam!" cried Joyce. The old man stopped and looked up. He smiled and waved at her. "Good morning!" he called. Joyce flew toward him. "I just saw the unicorn," she panted.

"Did you now?" Sam's green eyes were sparkling in his brown face. "That's wonderful. You must tell me all about it."

"Will do, but later!" she promised. "Got to dash!" She took off again but hadn't gone very far when she circled back around. "Oh, Sam! I nearly forgot," she cried, pulling the somewhat crushed pack of sandwiches from her bag. "Mom said to give you these, cheese and pickle, I think. Here, catch."

"Tell your mother thanks," said Sam as he deftly caught the packet, but Joyce was out of earshot by then.

When she reached the school, she ran straight in, thundered up the stairs, opened the third door on the left, and burst into her classroom. Her fellow students were standing at their desks unpacking their books from their bags. Amazingly, she wasn't late! Class had not yet started.

Joyce jumped on a chair. "Listen, everybody!" she yelled. "I saw the unicorn!"

Some of her classmates giggled, others rolled their eyes. One or two glanced nervously toward the front of the class. "I did, really! I saw him. He was drinking from the brook and his coat is pure white and his mane and tail are a beautiful pale gold, and he's the most amazing thing I have ever seen in my entire—"

The sound of a book being slammed down made her stop instantly. Joyce's shoulders shot up to her ears. Slowly she turned. Her teacher, Miss Crisp, was standing at the chalkboard, glaring at her. Joyce smiled weakly.

"Um, good morning, Miss Crisp," she said.

The teacher gave her a withering look. "Come here," she said. Laughter broke out amongst the other fairies. Miss Crisp banged her book down again. The laughter stopped. "The rest of you may go. Quietly! And remember, even though you'll be at home, this is still a school day. I expect you to spend every single moment studying. Is that understood?"

Joyce watched in bewilderment as her classmates filed out of the room.

Joyce grabbed a passing fairy. "What did I miss, Mel?" she whispered.

"We're being sent home to study for our end-of-term tests next week," Mel whispered back. "Crispers thinks we'll learn better in the quiet of our own homes."

"No talking. Keep moving," said Miss Crisp, clapping her hands. "Joyce, I'm waiting!"

Joyce reached the desk. "Well?" Miss Crisp asked when all the other fairies had left.

"Oh, miss, I'm sorry I was late but the unicorn was so beautiful—"

"Joyce!" snapped Miss Crisp, holding up her hand. "Unicorns? For goodness' sake. Please. I don't want to hear any more outlandish excuses for your tardiness!"

"Sorry, Miss Crisp," mumbled Joyce.

"And is 'sorry' good enough, Joyce?"

"No, miss."

" 'No' is right, Joyce. Now go home and study for your end-of-term exams like the others, and, as extra punishment, you can write me a ten-page essay about the evils of tardiness and bring it to me first thing in the morning!"

Joyce nodded and turned to go.

"And Joyce?" Miss Crisp called after her. "Sort out your wings. They look terrible!"

"Yes, miss."

Joyce hurried out of the room, down the steps, out the school door, and was about to head toward the market square when she remembered her promise to Sam. Joyce turned and headed away from the market, promising that she would absolutely, definitely go straight home and start studying, just as soon as she'd found Sam and told him all about the unicorn. She knew that Sam, unlike Crispers, would believe her.

Old Sam Swain may have just been a raggedy street sweeper, but he was one of the cleverest fairies Joyce had ever met, and he was a born teacher. He not only knew the names of the stars, but also of every plant, tree, flower, and even rock to be found in the forest. He could carve twigs into whistles, tie endlessly complicated knots, even catch fish with his bare hands, and, best of all, he knew how to tell stories, especially big people stories, in just the proper way. When Sam was telling a group of young fairies a story, even the most rambunctious ones sat still and listened. Sam never seemed to mind Joyce asking him about things. "It's important not to stop questioning," he often said. "How else will you learn about your world?"

Chapter 4

TALLYHO

While Joyce was hurrying to find Sam the street sweeper, much was happening in the world of big people. The magnificent medieval courtyard of Swinley Castle was teeming with some of the finest horseflesh in the country. The Royal hunt was scheduled to start in less than half an hour.

A Royal hunt is an event to which anyone who thinks they are *anyone* would like to be invited. Some of the more image-conscious guests act as though they find the whole thing a dreadful bore, but secretly they are ecstatic that they have been asked. It is the grandest and the most select "do" of its kind in the entire country—some say in the entire world.

In attendance at this hunt were the usual crowned heads of state, assorted politicians—disgraced and otherwise—and a few princes and princesses. There were dukes and duchesses, the odd earl, a number of honorable ladies, a smattering of pop stars and famous actors, a best-selling author (American), one or two opera singers, and an inordinate number of semi-famous media personalities, some of whom, or so it was rumored, only learned to ride so that they could be invited to the hunt.

Besides all of the above (and you can imagine the din—horses snorting, toffs braying, media types dropping names and blathering on about themselves) there were also dozens of grooms assisting the riders, tens of footmen carrying trays of stirrup cup, and an army of lady's maids to tend to their mistresses' attire.

In a far corner close to the stable door an excited Princess Eleanor, having bade the Master of the Hounds the customary "good morning," was now waiting for her mount to be brought out. Merrie stood on one side of her and her bodyguard, Captain Simperington, stood on the other.

Captain Simperington was a tall, handsome, and extremely capable ex-member of the Special Air

Services—the S.A.S. He was the ideal bodyguard—watchful, courteous, and, despite his immense size, extremely unobtrusive. He was a quiet man, sometimes so quiet the princess would forget he was there.

Now he stood beside her, immense and still in his red riding coat, jodhpurs, and shining black boots. His piercing blue-green eyes peered out from beneath the peak of his riding helmet and scanned the crowds for anything that might threaten the princess's safety.

"Your mount, Your Highness," he said, indicating a sweet-looking tubby yellow pony being led toward them by a groom.

The princess spun around. "Lemon!" she cried, rushing up and taking the reins. "Hello, my Lemon," she said as she kissed the pony's soft nose and fed her a sugar lump. "You look like a real hunter today!" Eleanor laughed, then turned to the groom and smiled. "Could you help me up please, Hobbs?" she asked. "Excited, Merrie?"

"I can hardly wait," said the governess, the edges of her jaw twitching. She touched a gloved finger to the bristles on her chin.

"You mustn't worry, Merrie," said the princess. "Really, don't. There's nothing to be scared of. We'll be hunting an aniseed trail, not a live fox, and we've found the perfect horse for you. Look."

She pointed to a groom who was struggling to gain control of a robust black stallion with a magnificent glossy black coat and wildly flaring nostrils. The governess staggered back.

Eleanor laughed. "Oh, no, Merrie, not him. That's The Bolter. A ride on him would put you off for life." The Bolter rolled his eyes so far back in his head that only the whites showed. "Simpers is riding him. You're on Mystery. Here she comes now."

Merrie looked vastly relieved when another groom emerged from the stables leading a small, placid, dun-colored mare.

The hounds yelped gleefully, and the huntsmen and huntswomen mounted their horses with varying degrees of elegance and ease. It took both grooms and a good deal of heaving and shoving to get Merrie up onto Mystery's back. Once there, she sat slumped over like a sack of potatoes, clutching desperately at the saddle. Captain Simperington, however, needed no help. He set a foot in The Bolter's stirrup and in one swift movement hoisted himself onto the magnificent animal's back.

The princess looked over at him to say something but he was talking quietly into the microphone hidden in his sleeve. She couldn't hear what he was saying but she knew he was probably talking to one of the guards. All the Royal bodyguards were issued the most cutting-edge surveillance equipment, but Simpers always seemed to have the most groundbreaking models. The earpiece he wore was so tiny that it was almost invisible to the naked eye, and the microphone secreted in his cuff was microscopically small.

Once everyone was mounted, the "horsey" riders checked their saddles and stirrups. The "non-horsey" ones tried to look confident and cool. The hunting horn sounded. Two long melodious notes quickly followed by two shorter ones told the riders it was time to leave the confines of the castle and make for the meadow. Now all the riders adjusted their cravats and gloves, slipped their booted feet into the stirrups, and, with a clicking of tongues and kicking of heels, began to steer their steeds through the main gate. They clip-clopped over the drawbridge and down the lane, toward the meadow where, at the sound of the huntsman's horn and the master's rallying cry, the Royal hunt would begin in earnest.

The princess rode beautifully. She had excellent posture, a good seat, and a natural, very Royal, affinity for horses. As the hunt moved toward the meadow, she sat relaxed and upright on Lemon's back, enjoying the view across the fields.

"What a lovely day, Your Highness," said Merrie.

Princess Eleanor could see that the governess was getting the hang of riding now. Mystery had a nice, easy gate and was very well behaved. "Oh, Your Highness, you were so right," Merrie went on. "This is fun."

Eleanor smiled at her governess and then turned her attention to the long line of riders in front of her. She could see her parents at the front, a long way ahead. It would be fun to catch up and ride with them, she thought. She missed her parents and wished she could be with them more often. That was the problem with having a king for a dad and a queen for a mom. They were away on state business a lot of the time, and even when they were at home, they were, as Merrie often told her, too busy with engagements to have much time to see her. They'd hardly even said hello to her that morning, just a brief wave and a kiss blown across the bustling courtyard. Eleanor had waved back and tried to smile brightly.

A sharp beep brought her back to the present. "Was that your phone, Merrie?" she asked, surprised that Merrie had brought her phone to a hunt.

Merrie smiled apologetically and, ineptly holding the reins with one hand, pulled the purple mobile out of her pocket. "Dear me, I didn't realize I'd brought it along," she said as she opened it up and read the message on the screen.

The princess leaned over. "Merrie!" she whispered. "Don't let the Master of the Hounds see you with that. I'm sure he'd say it's not good form to bring a phone on a hunt. And it could be dangerous if it rang—might spook your horse or someone else's. You'd better switch it off."

"Yes, you're absolutely right, my dear," agreed Merrie, smiling at her pupil as she closed the phone and slipped it back in her pocket. "I don't want to get in trouble. It's off now."

Eventually, when the field master (always the last rider) had joined the entire party of hounds, horses, and huntsmen and huntswomen assembled in a haphazard mass at the bottom of the meadow, the huntsman blew his horn. The hounds, having found the scent of the aniseed trail, took off over the grass with the keenest hunters thundering in their wake. The hunt was on.

The princess and her companions were about to set off behind the other hunters when suddenly Merrie's cell phone rang. As the princess had feared, the shrill sound spooked Merrie's horse. Mystery pricked up her ears, shook her head, and, with a suddenness that startled even the usually un-startle-able Simpers, shot off after the other horses. A moment later Mystery peeled off from the rest of the hunters and tore north-ward across the field. Pretty soon the crazed pony was heading off solo, speeding toward a large, impenetrable-looking hedge.

"Heeelllllllppp!" Merrie's scream was distant and thin.

Simpers and Eleanor watched with their mouths open as, with a gravity-defying leap, Mystery cleared the hedge, then dropped out of sight over the other side.

"We've got to go after her, Simpers!" cried the princess, recovering her senses. Captain Simpering-ton hesitated. "It's all right, Simps. You won't be leav-ing your post. I'll be right behind you."

Simpers nodded, kicked The Bolter's flanks, and charged after Merrie. Lemon tried to keep up; she was surprisingly quick for her size, but today she didn't have the speed. The princess realized some-thing must be wrong and pulled back on the reins.

"Whoa!" she cried. Lemon obediently stopped. Eleanor dismounted, then threw the reins over Lemon's head and led her around, intently watching how she walked. One thing was immediately appar-ent. Lemon was favoring her front right leg and limp-ing on her left.

"Poor Lemon. You must have bruised it," she said,

patting the pony's sweating neck. "No more galloping for you today." The princess shaded her eyes with her hand and stared back toward the castle. It was a long walk to the stables. She looked in the other direction. Two fields over she could see Merrie flailing wildly on Mystery's back as the pony galloped toward the horizon. Behind them, The Bolter was catching up. Eleanor didn't doubt that when Simpers had rescued Merrie, they would come and find her. "Don't worry, Lemon," she said. "I'll ask Simpers to have Hobbs bring the horse van for you. Let's find a shady place to sit till then."

Gently she led the limping Lemon up the slope toward Swinley Forest. When they reached the trees, Princess Eleanor lay down at the foot of a great sycamore and smiled as she stared up into the glorious canopy of leaves.

Chapter 5

REASONS

"Sam!" cried Joyce as she ran. "Sam!"

The old street sweeper turned and waved, then leaned on his broom handle and waited. Most fairies in Swinley Hope thought Sam was a bit touched in the head because he was so quiet and seemed content to sweep the streets for a living. They always said it was a shame. The old fairies remembered him as such a bright and lively lad, and so clever. Everyone had thought he would be chief alder one day, and he would have been, if only he hadn't gone adventuring beyond the forest. He was never quite the same after that. Before he left, his hair had been as black as midnight, but when he returned after seventeen summers, it was pure white. They said it was the shock of what he saw that did it, but Sam just laughed when he heard this.

Sam was the only fairy who'd ever gone beyond the forest, but he never talked about it. These were the only questions of Joyce's that he wouldn't answer, and he wouldn't say why he wouldn't, either. This made Joyce all the more curious. The outside world intrigued her, and she couldn't understand why no one else was interested. When she asked her father if he'd ever wanted to go beyond the forest, he confessed that, like most fairies he knew, he'd never given it much thought.

"Joycey, my love," he'd said. "The forest is plenty big enough for me. I have your mom and you, and your sisters; I have my friends and my work; we've got plenty to eat, and it's a beautiful place to live. Why would I ever want to leave?" Joyce couldn't answer that. All the fairies she knew were happy to spend their entire lives in Swinley Hope. They would work in the forest or the town just as their parents and grandparents had before them. They never asked what lay beyond the forest. They probably hadn't even wondered about it. Joyce had, though. She'd wondered about it a lot. She knew the forest was an amazing place to live, but sometimes . . .

Joyce ran full pelt down the street. When she'd almost caught up to him, Sam picked up his broom.

"Let's walk you home and you can tell me everything," he said, smiling and setting off. Joyce fell into step beside him.

"Oh, Sam, he was so beautiful," she began when she'd got her breath back. "I've never ever seen anything half so lovely in my whole life." Then she went on, describing the unicorn in the minutest detail, from the color of his mane to the length of his eyelashes, while Sam listened thoughtfully. They were almost at her tree before she'd finished her tale. "The thing I don't understand, though," she mused as they reached the steps, "is why the unicorn came so close to town. He's never done that before, has he?"

Sam stopped and regarded her with his piercing green eyes, and then he gazed far into the dark forest. "Perhaps he wanted you to see him," he said quietly.

Joyce was mystified. "Why?" she asked.

"He'll have his reasons," Sam replied. "Though I doubt we'll ever learn what they are." Suddenly he shook himself. "I'd better get to work," he announced abruptly. "These streets won't sweep themselves. Be

40

seeing you, Joyce." And with that he marched off down the street.

Joyce hurried home, bounding up the steps of her tree. With exams to study for and an extra essay to write, she had no time to waste.

As soon as she was home, she shut herself in her bedroom, carefully spread her books and her notes on the little desk by the window, sat down, and began to study. She almost managed to do it for a full minute before her mind started to wander. She just couldn't concentrate. It's too stuffy in here, she thought. I need fresh air. Perhaps a little exercise before I settle down.

This thought had barely entered her mind before she was climbing over her table and crawling out of her window onto the branch. The sounds and smells of the market drifted up. The dust hung in the still air, and the sunlight lit it prettily.

Joyce took a deep breath, stretched her wings, and smiled as she thought about the unicorn. She'd have given just about anything to see him again.

The unicorn had been drinking at the brook, and as he'd probably need to drink more than once a day, especially in the summer, he'd have to go to the brook to drink quite often.

She could, she thought, just spend a few minutes looking for him, couldn't she?

She spread her wings and dove off the branch, letting herself free-fall for a moment before swooping up into the leaves. She soon reached the brook and began to follow it into the forest.

When she'd flown a little way downstream and had still seen no sign of the unicorn, she began to think she was being a little foolish. Who was she kidding? Seeing the unicorn once in a lifetime was amazing. Twice had to be impossible, except . . .

What was that in the darkness? It looked like the flash of a golden hoof catching a thin shaft of sunlight. Joyce didn't hesitate. She flew after it as fast as her wings could carry her.

Soon she was farther from the village than any forest fairy had been in a long, long time. She didn't notice. Her eyes were fixed on the distant tantalizing glimpses of the speeding animal as it hurtled through the forest ahead of her. Then all of a sudden he was gone.

Joyce landed on a branch and waited for her heart to stop pounding so hard. She looked around and was relieved to see the brook was only a little way off. She'd be able to follow that back to town.

BLAHHHHHHHH! A loud jarring noise interrupted her thoughts. BLAHHHHHHHH!

Joyce sat bolt upright. What was that?

Then came one long note that was followed by a sort of whooping staccato succession of shorter notes. BLAHHH BLA BLA BLAAAAAHHHHH!

She peered through the trees in the direction of the sound. She could see nothing but the dense thicket. She could hear other strange sounds now, a mix of chattering and champing and stamping and braying—it sounded a little like the sounds from the market, and she began to wonder if she'd flown in a circle and was heading back home. The blaring horn sounded again loud and clear. That definitely wasn't coming from the village. She set off toward the sound.

Suddenly she shot out into . . . nothing. There were no more trees. Joyce had flown into a place so bright that it blinded her. She covered her face with her hands and, somewhat panic-stricken, hovered in place.

"It's all right," she told herself. "It's all right." Keeping her eyes tightly closed, she slowly lowered her hands. The light was astonishingly bright. She opened her eyes a fraction. Everything was green. Not the dark cool greens of the forest, but a bright light green, brighter than the velvet on an alderman's cap. It was so bright it made her head ache. She shut her eyes and tried again to calm herself down.

"It's all right," she muttered again. But was it? She

knew exactly where she was. She had flown all the way to the edge of the forest! She opened her eyes again, just a fraction. Her pupils were growing more accustomed to the brightness, and it was not quite as hard this time to look.

In front of her lay a great expanse of bright green grass. It was beautiful. Joyce flew down to get a closer look. In amongst the grasses there were all manner of plants and flowers she'd never seen before.

She flew to the nearest tree and sat on a thin branch. The sky was enormous. She had only ever seen a little of it at a time through the leaves, and even in the wintertime when the trees were bare, the twigs were so dense that the sky wasn't all that easy to see beyond them. But here there was such a great and wonderful expanse of blue, and on the horizon sat vast puffy clouds.

On top of the hill far across the green valley stood a huge edifice made of golden-hued stone. A bright flag flapped on a flagpole on the top of the highest roof. Joyce wondered what this place could be. Before she could work it out, her attention was caught by the sound of dogs barking. She squinted across the grass in the direction of the sound. She had been so busy staring at the big sky and the other marvels of this place that she hadn't even noticed the group of figures on horseback assembled in the meadow.

"Oh!" Joyce gasped with excitement. "Other fairies!" There were so many of them. Some were wearing red coats and some were wearing black and all of them were riding fairy horses—blacks and chestnuts, bays and grays—while a pack of fairy dogs sniffed around in the grass.

But as Joyce stared at the group, she realized that something about them didn't seem quite right.

The horn sounded again. Joyce could see that it was one of the riders at the front of the group who was blowing it. The sun glinted on the brass horn as its notes sang out across the valley. Suddenly the dogs were off, barking wildly and wagging their tails furiously. The horses followed, and the air was filled with the thunderous thudding of their galloping hooves. Joyce covered her ears with her hands.

Within seconds all the dogs and the horses were galloping over the hillside and out of sight. Before they disappeared, a small horse at the back of the pack broke free and veered off in another direction. The little figure on its back bounced around like a rag doll. Two riders set off after this first and were gaining ground until one horse, the smaller of the two, slowed and stopped in the middle of the grass while the other galloped on and followed the runaway through a hedge.

Joyce watched the horse that had stopped. The rider dismounted and walked the horse around. After a few turns they started up the slope and headed toward Joyce's tree.

Then something incredible started to happen. Joyce watched in astonishment as the rider and horse grew bigger and bigger and bigger. Soon they were twice the size they'd been when she first spotted them, and they were still growing. By the time they reached the foot of Joyce's tree, they looked at least ten times as big as a fairy. Joyce's mouth felt dry and her hands were sticky and she felt sick and excited and scared all at the same time. She could no longer ignore the fact that this enormous creature was—for what other explanation could there be?—an actual big person.

Big people are REAL! a voice screamed inside her head. Her mom was right. BIG PEOPLE ARE REAL! And they are VERY, VERY BIG!

Chapter 6

THE ROYAL SNEEZE

Joyce was breathing very fast, and her heart was thumping in her chest. There was a big person sitting at the bottom of the very tree in which she was sitting. Could this really be happening? She closed her eyes and then opened them. The big person was still there. She pinched her knee and squeezed hard to see if she was awake and wasn't really sprawled over her botany book with a sticky puddle of drool seeping under her cheek. She squeezed harder. Ow! She was definitely awake.

What, Joyce wondered, would Sam say when she

told him about— SAM! She laughed. Of course Sam already knew big people were real, didn't he? He must have seen them on his travels, which was why his stories were always full of such riveting details. Joyce gazed down from her tree.

Below her, the big person took off her hat and let loose a lot of long blond hair. Joyce watched, mesmerized.

Joyce saw the girl drop the horse's reins.

"Go on, Lemon," the girl said kindly. "You eat while I enjoy the peace and quiet." Then she lay down under the tree and smiled up at the leaves. Instinctively Joyce ducked behind a leaf. The girl sighed loudly and put her hands behind her head. "Lovely," she said as she closed her eyes and lay there very still.

Joyce watched her for some time, but the girl didn't move. She just stayed like that, her chest rising and falling and the breeze gently blowing her golden hair.

Joyce wanted to get a closer look at the girl, but she hesitated. If big people were real, which they obviously were, it meant the stories were true. Gruesome details popped into her mind—big people tortured fairies!

She remembered how Sam had said that it was mostly only the youngest big people, babies and such, who could actually see fairies. Joyce stared down at the girl. She looked young, but she was far from being a baby. Of course, Sam had also said that some grown ones kept the gift all their lives. Joyce thought about it. It was risky, but if she was going to go in closer, she needed somewhere to hide. She looked around and saw an almost perfect place.

A neighboring tree had a low branch that crossed toward where the girl lay and ended directly above her nose. To make it even more perfect, the branch had an unruly cluster of leaves sticking out of the end of it. If she could just get to those leaves and hide there, she would be able to get a closer look and still stay hidden. Quietly, Joyce flew up through the leaves above her, crossed to the neighboring tree, then made her way to the low branch.

She was just negotiating her way around the clump of leaves when the girl on the ground sneezed so loud that Joyce lost her balance. She screamed as she plummeted toward the enormous face.

It took an incredible effort and much strenuous flapping of her wings to stop herself from crashing right into the girl's nose, but somehow she managed it. Just.

Then the girl opened her eyes.

Joyce hovered in the air inches above the girl's

face, watching in horror as the two huge bright blue eyes blinked once, twice, and then a third time.

"Oh!" exclaimed the girl.

The girl's breath hit Joyce like a warm, sweet wind. Joyce flapped her wings and shot toward the trees. To her horror, the girl leapt up and chased her.

Once in the woods Joyce darted to her right, landed on a sycamore tree, and hid behind a leaf. Peeking out, she watched the girl pass by below and stop abruptly. Why was she stopping? The girl was standing absolutely still in the undergrowth. She had her back to Joyce and was staring at something in the woods.

"How beautiful!" the girl gasped.

Joyce flew down to the next branch to get a better look, and tears sprang into her eyes.

"No!" she cried.

The unicorn of Swinley Forest was standing in the bracken a few yards in front of the girl.

The princess had never seen such a magnificent animal. He was not much taller than Lemon, but he was no pony. From the perfect shape of his magnificent head, the astonishingly white coat, and the strong, elegant curve of his neck, she would have said he was the purest of thoroughbreds, but the gleaming golden horn on his forehead made him something else entirely.

"Are you real?" asked the princess softly.

The unicorn tossed his head and whinnied.

Afraid that he might run away, Eleanor cautiously repositioned herself so that she was no longer facing him full on. It was how she'd been taught to act around skittish horses.

The unicorn's ears shot forward; he took a couple of steps toward her, then stopped and pawed the ground with a golden hoof. The princess stayed where she was, her relaxed body language inviting him to come and see her.

"It's all right," she said softly. "I wouldn't do anything to hurt you."

Haltingly, he walked up to her and, lowering his head, blew his breath through his nose. The princess understood. Taking care not to frighten him, Princess Eleanor walked forward with the quiet confidence she knew to use around horses. She stopped by his shoulder; then, making her movements slow and easy for him to see, she gently stroked his beautiful neck. The unicorn craned his head around, rested his chin on her shoulder, and nuzzled her neck.

From her perch in the tree Joyce watched in dismay. The unicorn and the girl had only just met, but they looked as if they'd been friends forever.

Just then two fairies flew into the clearing. One landed on the broad branch of a sycamore tree, two along from hers. The other zipped around the inner edge of the clearing. Joyce stared from one fairy to the other. They were definitely not from the forest. For one thing they were flying, and for another they both wore charcoal-colored suits, white shirts, thin black ties, and dark glasses. One had extremely short black hair; the other's was red and was worn even shorter. Their wings were long and muscular and shone like polished chrome. The one who was circling the clearing flew with a speed and efficiency that Joyce could never have imagined. As he flew, his eyes scanned everything searchingly.

Joyce ducked behind the nearest leaf as he whizzed toward her tree. As he sped by, the wind from his wings shook the leaf she was hiding behind. Joyce held on tight to the stalk and the fairy passed by without seeing her. When he'd gone, she peeked out and saw him land beside the other fairy on the tree branch. Once there, he took out a pair of small binoculars and trained them on the princess. His partner stood a little way off and appeared to be talking into his hand.

A moment later Joyce heard a deep voice call: "Your Highness?"

back to the castle with you. That way you could see him all day, every day. He could live in the Royal stables, have every modern comfort, and you'd be there with him anytime you wanted. Wouldn't you just love that?"

The princess was silent for a moment. "Yes," she said thoughtfully. "I would like that very much."

"Then there's no problemo, my sweet," said Merrie, smiling so wide that she showed an unpleasant amount of her gums.

"But . . ." The princess hesitated. "There's just . . . it doesn't feel like something we should—"

"Oh, my dear," Merrie gushed, "anyone with eyes can see how he adores you. Besides, it doesn't have to be forever. You can always bring him back here if he's unhappy."

The princess's face lit up. She went up to the unicorn and scratched him under his chin.

"What do you think? Do you want to come home with me?"

The unicorn pushed at her gently with his nose, then swished his tail and pawed impatiently at the ground with a golden hoof. The princess grinned a big, happy grin. "All right, my unicorn," she laughed. "Let's go home."

The unicorn jerked his head away from the girl's shoulder and switched his tail. He stepped back. The girl reached up and stroked his neck.

"Shhssshh," she cooed, smoothing down his mane. "It's all right, it's just Simpers. He's a friend. Don't worry, he won't hurt you. Shuushhh."

A large man, a gigantic man more than twice as tall as the girl, stepped into the clearing.

He gave a little bow. "Your Highness," he said.

The unicorn eyed the man nervously, but the girl's hand on his neck steadied him.

"Hello, Simpers," she said. "This is my new friend. He's a unicorn. Isn't he beautiful?"

"Yes, miss, he is," agreed the big man.

A few moments later another big person stumbled into the clearing. This one was a woman—bone thin with red lips and coppery hair. She looked panic-stricken and very out of breath.

"Princess Baby!" the woman puffed as she staggered toward the girl. "My . . . darling . . . my sweet . . . I was so . . . worried . . . when I saw your pony standing all alone at the edge of the forest, and there was no sign of you . . . and Captain Simperington quickly examined Lemon, looking for clues, and said he was lame. Now come along. And don't worry, the captain called Hobbs to bring a horse van across the meadow to pick up poor lame Lem— ARGGGHHH!" The bony woman screamed as the unicorn dashed out of nowhere and rose up, hooves flailing in front of her. She fell back in the bracken, then, shrieking all the while, she scrambled across the ground on all fours and hid behind the nearest tree trunk.

The girl strode up to the unicorn and ducked under his neck. "No, no," she chided him gently. "You can't do that, silly. That's Merrie. She's not going to hurt you. She's a friend, too. Aren't you, Merrie?"

The bony woman peeked around the tree, staring openmouthed at the unicorn, a dazed look on her face. "Um . . . Your . . . Highness . . . what is . . . um . . . is that . . . is that a . . . oh goodness . . . please . . . is that a . . . ?"

The girl's grin grew even wider. "Yes, Merrie, he's a unicorn! Isn't he lovely?"

The bony woman nodded even more and slid back down to the ground.

Princess Eleanor was happy to see that it didn't take long for Simpers to gain, at least partially, the unicorn's trust. Captain Simperington was a natural horseman, and the unicorn soon allowed him to stand a little closer, even to approach him.

Merrie, on the other hand, stayed put. No matter how many times the princess asked her to come meet the unicorn, the governess refused.

"No, no, my pet, you enjoy yourself," she replied, getting to her feet. "Honestly, I'm perfectly content watching you and your new friend. How happy you look. Though it really is time we were going. Hobbs will be waiting for us to take Lemon back."

"Very well, Merrie," replied the princess.

Merrie smiled. "You can come back tomorrow to see your unicorn."

The princess grinned. "Yes. Good idea. I'll do that." She patted the unicorn and gently kissed his cheek. "I'll see you tomorrow," she promised. "And I'll bring you some of my extra delicious sugar carrots—I roll them in brown sugar. Yum! Lemon loves them."

The unicorn touched his nose to Eleanor's shoulder and nibbled at her ear. The princess giggled. "Come on, Simps," she said. "Let's go and see about Lemon."

The princess was halfway across the clearing when she felt the unicorn nudge her in the back. He shook his head playfully when she turned.

"No, no, no!" She laughed. "Stay here. I'll see you tomorrow."

"You know, Your Highness," Merrie suggested thoughtfully, "you could, if you like, take your unicorn

The unicorn jerked his head away from the girl's shoulder and switched his tail. He stepped back. The girl reached up and stroked his neck.

"Shhssshh," she cooed, smoothing down his mane. "It's all right, it's just Simpers. He's a friend. Don't worry, he won't hurt you. Shuushhh."

A large man, a gigantic man more than twice as tall as the girl, stepped into the clearing.

He gave a little bow. "Your Highness," he said.

The unicorn eyed the man nervously, but the girl's hand on his neck steadied him.

"Hello, Simpers," she said. "This is my new friend. He's a unicorn. Isn't he beautiful?"

"Yes, miss, he is," agreed the big man.

A few moments later another big person stumbled into the clearing. This one was a woman—bone thin with red lips and coppery hair. She looked panic-stricken and very out of breath.

"Princess Baby!" the woman puffed as she staggered toward the girl. "My . . . darling . . . my sweet . . . I was so . . . worried . . . when I saw your pony standing all alone at the edge of the forest, and there was no sign of you . . . and Captain Simperington quickly examined Lemon, looking for clues, and said he was lame. Now come along. And don't worry, the captain called Hobbs to bring a horse van across the meadow to pick up poor lame Lem— ARGGGHHH!" The bony woman screamed as the unicorn dashed out of nowhere and rose up, hooves flailing in front of her. She fell back in the bracken, then, shrieking all the while, she scrambled across the ground on all fours and hid behind the nearest tree trunk.

The girl strode up to the unicorn and ducked under his neck. "No, no," she chided him gently. "You can't do that, silly. That's Merrie. She's not going to hurt you. She's a friend, too. Aren't you, Merrie?"

The bony woman peeked around the tree, staring openmouthed at the unicorn, a dazed look on her face. "Um . . . Your . . . Highness . . . what is . . . um . . . is that . . . is that a . . . oh goodness . . . please . . . is that a . . . ?"

The girl's grin grew even wider. "Yes, Merrie, he's a unicorn! Isn't he lovely?"

The bony woman nodded even more and slid back down to the ground.

Princess Eleanor was happy to see that it didn't take long for Simpers to gain, at least partially, the unicorn's trust. Captain Simperington was a natural horseman, and the unicorn soon allowed him to stand a little closer, even to approach him.

Merrie, on the other hand, stayed put. No matter how many times the princess asked her to come meet the unicorn, the governess refused.

"No, no, my pet, you enjoy yourself," she replied, getting to her feet. "Honestly, I'm perfectly content watching you and your new friend. How happy you look. Though it really is time we were going. Hobbs will be waiting for us to take Lemon back."

"Very well, Merrie," replied the princess.

Merrie smiled. "You can come back tomorrow to see your unicorn."

The princess grinned. "Yes. Good idea. I'll do that." She patted the unicorn and gently kissed his cheek. "I'll see you tomorrow," she promised. "And I'll bring you some of my extra delicious sugar carrots—I roll them in brown sugar. Yum! Lemon loves them."

The unicorn touched his nose to Eleanor's shoulder and nibbled at her ear. The princess giggled. "Come on, Simps," she said. "Let's go and see about Lemon."

The princess was halfway across the clearing when she felt the unicorn nudge her in the back. He shook his head playfully when she turned.

"No, no, no!" She laughed. "Stay here. I'll see you tomorrow."

"You know, Your Highness," Merrie suggested thoughtfully, "you could, if you like, take your unicorn back to the castle with you. That way you could see him all day, every day. He could live in the Royal stables, have every modern comfort, and you'd be there with him anytime you wanted. Wouldn't you just love that?"

The princess was silent for a moment. "Yes," she said thoughtfully. "I would like that very much."

"Then there's no problemo, my sweet," said Merrie, smiling so wide that she showed an unpleasant amount of her gums.

"But . . ." The princess hesitated. "There's just . . . it doesn't feel like something we should—"

"Oh, my dear," Merrie gushed, "anyone with eyes can see how he adores you. Besides, it doesn't have to be forever. You can always bring him back here if he's unhappy."

The princess's face lit up. She went up to the unicorn and scratched him under his chin.

"What do you think? Do you want to come home with me?"

The unicorn pushed at her gently with his nose, then swished his tail and pawed impatiently at the ground with a golden hoof. The princess grinned a big, happy grin. "All right, my unicorn," she laughed. "Let's go home."

Up in her tree Joyce watched as the big people and the two charcoal-suited fairies left the clearing. She felt sick as she saw the unicorn follow the girl into the trees. What was she going to do? Without the unicorn, Swinley Forest and everything in it would die.

Chapter 7

The Alarm

Joyce flew faster than she had ever flown before. She kicked at the air with her feet and swerved through the trees as she followed the brook all the way back to Swinley Hope.

It was early afternoon when she reached the town. Without caring what anyone thought, she flew up this avenue and down that, all the while searching for any sign of the old street sweeper, but she couldn't see him anywhere. She was flying over the market square when she heard her mother shouting at her.

"JOYCE! Get down here at once!" She didn't look pleased. Joyce flew straight down and landed. Her mother was furious. "For heaven's sakes, Joyce," she said in an angry whisper. Passersby shook their heads and tutted. Her mother looked harassed. "What on earth were you—"

Joyce burst out crying. Her mother immediately stopped being angry and became concerned. She gathered Joyce up in her arms and held her close. "Sweetheart, what is it? What's happened?"

"Oh, Mom," Joyce blurted between great heaving sobs. "I saw them, three of them, and they—"

"Hush, my darling, it doesn't matter," said her mom. "Let's get you home and we'll have a proper talk." But Joyce was too distressed, and now that she'd started she wanted to tell her mom everything. Unfortunately, she didn't realize that her loud sobs were attracting a lot of attention.

"They were in the forest," she wailed. "And they . . . and they—"

Her mom pulled away and held Joyce at arms' length. She studied her face. "Joycey, my love, you're not making any sense. Who was in the forest?"

"The big people!" replied Joyce. "The Bigguns! They were here in the woods and they . . . and they . . . oh, Mom, it was all my fault!"

Joyce dissolved into tears again, and her mother hugged her close. "Hush, my darling, hush."

But the group of eavesdroppers surrounding them had heard what Joyce had said. "What was that?" they whispered. "What did she say? Bigguns? Bigguns in the forest? BIGGUNS!"

Within moments the whisperers were no longer whispering, they were shouting. Joyce's news spread rapidly through the market square and all over the town. BIGGUNS IN THE FOREST! BIGGUNS IN THE FOREST! Suddenly every fairy in Swinley Hope had forgotten that they'd stopped believing in big people. All the ancient terrors were awakened in them. Big people were coming!

Joyce looked up from her mother's shoulder and saw all sorts of fairies rushing about. Their alarmed faces frightened her. "What's happening?" she asked. Her mother put her arm around her shoulder.

"Let's get home, darling," she said, leading her away. Joyce noticed the tremble in her mother's normally calm voice.

A bell began to toll. It wasn't like the school bell. This was just one loud, somber note that sounded over and over again. Joyce had never heard this bell before, but she knew what it was. It was the bell that rang only when the town was in danger.

The Alder Fairies hurried through the crowd on

their way to the town hall, calling out instructions as they went.

"Get home! Hide everything!" they shouted.

In the square, fairies hurried to dismantle the market. The sound of bark shutters shutting echoed through the town. SLAM! SLAM! SLAM! The town was disappearing fast. Soon only the pub, the Twisted Elm, was still visible. Joyce could see the landlord urging four inebriated and protesting elves inside.

Everyone was trying to get home. Fairies who hadn't flown since they were children were flapping their wings and trying vainly to launch themselves into the air, but their beautiful flimsy wings couldn't carry them very far. Many gave up and ran as fast as they could and tried to climb up the already clogged stairways on the trees.

Joyce and her mother had almost reached their home tree when Joyce heard someone calling her name. She turned and saw Alderman Choosy coming toward her. He did not look happy.

"Tell me exactly what you saw," he said in a quiet voice when he joined them.

Joyce's mom put her arm around her shoulder. "Go on, love," she said gently.

Summoning all her courage, Joyce told how she'd seen the unicorn that morning by the brook and how she'd gone to look for him again. She skipped the part about how she flew to the edge of the forest and how the girl saw her and chased her, partly because she didn't want her mom to hear she'd gone so far from home and partly because she was ashamed. Instead she told the alder that she'd first seen the girl in the clearing looking at the unicorn. She told them how the unicorn and the girl had stared at each other, and then she paused, afraid to go on with her story, afraid to tell him what she knew she must: that the unicorn had left the forest with the big people.

Joyce heard her mother gasp when she told them, but Alderman Choosy didn't say a word. He simply stared at Joyce, then at her mom, then back at her. It felt like a long time before he spoke.

"The alders are meeting at the town hall," he murmured, as though talking to himself. "I must tell them." He looked up at Joyce's mother. "Take her home," he told her. "We will send for her if we have further questions." He turned and hurried off toward the town hall.

"Don't worry," said Joyce's mom as she steered her to the steps of their home tree. "The alders will find a way to bring the unicorn back, I'm sure they will." But Joyce could tell from her mother's voice that she wasn't sure at all.

That afternoon Margaret Merrieweather did something she had never done before. She gave the princess the entire afternoon off from her lessons and encouraged her to spend the hours till supper in the Royal stables with the newly installed unicorn and his tubby stallmate, Lemon. The princess was overjoyed. She could think of no better way to spend an afternoon than with her extraordinary new friend.

Hobbs had been waiting for them with a horse van when they'd emerged from the forest. The groom had been surprised to see they had a real unicorn with them, but after a quiet word from Captain Simperington, Hobbs, being a discreet and loyal fellow, had dutifully swallowed his surprise and got on with loading the animals.

When they'd arrived at the castle, Hobbs had backed the horse van all the way up the stable block and put Lemon and the unicorn well out of the way, in the very last stall.

Merrie gave Hobbs strict orders. No one but Hobbs, Captain Simperington, Her Highness, or Merrie herself was to go anywhere near the unicorn's stall. All the other grooms were to keep well away, and just in case anyone came snooping, she instructed

Hobbs to cover the bars of the stall with thick sack-cloth and stand guard all night.

"No one must know about your unicorn," Merrie told the princess. "It is imperative that we keep his existence a secret. Can you imagine what would happen if the press got wind of him?" Merrie shuddered. The princess agreed with her. It would be disastrous if word of the unicorn got out.

All afternoon Eleanor worked hard to make sure the unicorn got settled in happily. She helped Hobbs muck out the stall and lay fresh straw. She brought Lemon into the stall and then brushed her till her yellow coat shone. She filled the feed buckets and changed the water in the trough. When this was done, she fetched Lemon's tack, then sat on a stool and polished every bit of it. As she worked, she talked and talked to the unicorn, telling him anything she thought he might like to hear, and the unicorn stood quietly by, listening to her every word.

"Don't worry, I'll be back in the morning," she said when it was time for her to leave. The unicorn whinnied softly. "Good night, Lemon," the princess called to the pony in the corner. "And good night, my unicorn." She pulled the sacking curtain back over the bars and skipped happily all the way down the long aisle of the stable block as she headed to the castle for supper.

Chapter 8

AN ADVENTURE

Joyce didn't know exactly how long she'd sat there on the branch thinking, but when at last she stirred and leaned back to peer up through the leaves, she saw the sky was streaked with pink and gold clouds. It was sunset.

Joyce sighed. She'd been thinking all afternoon, but she hadn't come up with a way to make things better. How could she bring the unicorn back to the forest? She had to do something. But what? The answer came to her suddenly.

"Someone must go and find him and bring him back," she said out loud.

"Then you'd best be on your way, hadn't you?"

Joyce spun around and found Sam standing a few yards away, leaning against another branch.

"Me? Go?" sputtered Joyce. "That's impossible. How would I ever find him? I didn't see very much beyond the trees, nothing but sky and grass, oh, and there was a huge stone building on the h—" Joyce stopped, suddenly realizing what she was saying. She hadn't told anyone she'd gone to the edge of the forest. She glanced up at Sam and saw at once that he knew. "Oh, Sam," she said quietly. "That princess girl wouldn't have even seen the unicorn if I hadn't been so stupid."

Sam sat beside her. "What happened?" he asked. Joyce told him the whole story.

When she'd finished, he got to his feet, slapped the dust from his worn workman's trousers, and held out his hand to help her up. "Come on, you've no time to lose. Best be on your way."

Joyce blinked up at him. "But—but I can't go . . . ," she stammered.

"You have to," replied Sam, grasping her arm and pulling her to her feet. "The alders sent me here to tell you to."

"But why me?"

"Because you're the only one who can. None of

the others have your wing power. Did you see those fairies try to fly today? They couldn't do it. You flew all the way to the edge of the forest. No one else could do that. You must go, Joyce. It's not just for the forest's sake that you've got to bring him back, it's for the unicorn's, too. The forest won't survive without the unicorn, but the unicorn can't live for long outside his forest."

"But I don't know where they've taken him—"

"Then you'll have to find out," he replied. "It shouldn't be too difficult. You like asking questions."

"But—"

"Oh, for goodness' sake!" He suddenly laughed. "Don't you want to go?"

Joyce blinked at him.

"Don't I *want* to go?" she whispered.

Sam gazed out at the trees and his eyes took on a faraway look. "You've no idea how big the world is, Joyce," he said softly. "You've only seen the tiniest bit of it today, and I bet that meadow looked impossibly vast to you. But that's just the start of it. The great stone building you saw on the hill is a castle—it's a sort of house, only far bigger. And beyond that castle there's towns and villages stuffed full of all sorts of fairies and humans."

"Humans?" asked Joyce.

Sam smiled. "That's what they call Bigguns out there. Humans. They're a rum lot. You'll have to be careful. Some of them, like that blond girl, might be able to see you, but don't worry, that type are few and far between. Most of them won't have a clue you're there at all. On the whole they tend to be too busy to spot us flitting about. It's astounding that, big as they are, most of them never see what's right under their noses." Sam paused. "I envy you, Joyce. You'll see things on your journey that you could never have imagined. You'll meet fascinating and extraordinary fairies and humans. It'll be a fine adventure."

A fine *adventure*? Joyce hadn't thought of it like that. Leaving the forest to find the unicorn was a terrifying idea. On the other hand, if she thought of it as an *adventure*? She was quiet for a moment. They'd probably taken the unicorn to that stone castle on the hill. That hadn't looked so very far away. She could probably make it there, but it would mean crossing the sky. She looked up at the tiny patches of sunset that showed through the dark leaves and remembered how terrifyingly big the sky had looked at the edge of the forest. Sam guessed what she was thinking.

"You mustn't be afraid," he said. "I've never heard of a fairy being frazzled by the sun or blown away by the wind. Those are just stories to keep the little ones from straying too far from home. The only thing you have to be wary of is the rain, but that's the same in the forest as it is out there."

Joyce nodded thoughtfully. All she had to do was find the unicorn and bring him back. But it was a daunting task to undertake by herself.

"Couldn't you come, too?" she asked.

Sam shook his head. "Can't do it," he said. "My wings are too old to carry me far. Just flying up here to see you was an effort. Now listen carefully. Travel fast and light and don't dillydally or get sidetracked. You won't have time for that and you must not forget your purpose. Remember, the forest will be suffering. You must find the unicorn and bring him home."

"But how . . . how can I?" Joyce stammered as the physical impossibility of this suddenly occurred to her. "He's so big and I'm so small."

"Don't fret about that now. When the time comes, you'll find a way," Sam assured her. "Just have faith." He handed her a small canvas bag. "Take this. It's not much—water and a bit of grub—but it will keep you going till you find more." He clapped his hands together. "Right," he declared. "It's getting dark. Don't go through the woods, too dangerous in this light. You'd best fly up and travel above the trees. Go on, off you go."

"But I can't just go," protested Joyce. "I have to tell my parents."

"No need," he said. "The alders have already told them. Remember, this is official business."

Joyce nodded as Sam's tone reminded her how serious this was. She looped his bag over her shoulder and stared up through the leaves. She'd always wanted to fly above the treetops. She took a deep breath, flapped her wings, then pushed off with her feet and sped up between the leaves.

"Good luck," called Sam, but Joyce was already moving too fast to hear.

A few moments later she flew out into the darkening sky. The summer air was warm and still. Joyce looked down. Below her the dark forest appeared to be one vast, endless mass, offering no clue as to which way she should go. She would have to fly higher to get a better view.

High above her, the first stars were twinkling. Joyce flew toward them, reveling in the sensation of flying through such unobstructed space. Soon she was high enough to see the huge castle on the distant hill, lit bright as a winter fire. It didn't look so very far away. She beat her wings in a steady rhythm and headed toward it.

Chapter 9

The Royal Diary

Princess Eleanor's bedroom was very pink. The carpet was pink, the bedspread was pink, the curtains were pink, the furniture was pink, and the few things that weren't pink were gilded with a pinkish-gold gilt. Merrie, who had taken charge of the décor, had been extremely impressed with the results. She thought pink was perfect for a princess.

The princess's bed was massive and luxurious. Ten feet above it there hung an ornate canopy, fashioned into a gilded crown. Rich silk curtains, each a different shade of pink, swept elegantly down to curl around golden hooks on the wall at either side of the

Royal bed. On the bed itself sat a vast array of taffeta and brocade cushions in dazzlingly different hues of pink. These cushions were arranged at the head of the bed in order of size, the smallest ones at the front and the largest, squidgiest ones at the back.

Now wearing pink satin pajamas and a pink velvet dressing gown, Princess Eleanor sat cross-legged in the middle of her bed staring at nothing in particular.

"Why so thoughtful, my Princess Baby?" asked Merrie as she arranged the cushions on a chair.

"I was thinking about my unicorn," replied Eleanor.

"That's nice, dear—oh, my heavens!" she suddenly shrieked. "Just look at the time. Half past eight! Time to brush your teeth, Your Highness."

Obediently Eleanor hurried to the bathroom and picked up her pink toothbrush. As she brushed her teeth, she thought about how she'd first seen the unicorn and suddenly remembered something she'd completely forgotten about in all the excitement.

She'd been dozing on the grass when she'd sneezed and opened her eyes and seen something hovering above her nose. At first she'd thought it was a dragonfly, but as her eyes had focused, it had started to look less like a dragonfly and more like an impossibly small girl with wings. A fairy had been her first thought, but was it? She hadn't had a chance to find out; she'd lost it in the woods, and then she'd seen the unicorn and forgotten all about it until now.

"Are you coming, my darling?" called Merrie from the other room. The princess rinsed out her mouth and put her toothbrush away, then went back to the bedroom.

Merrie had turned down the covers. All the cushions had disappeared and had been replaced with large pink pillows. The governess sat beside the bed, holding a sleek black laptop on her knee. Eleanor's face fell when she saw it.

"Oh, not the diary," she said as she crawled into bed. "Do we have to?"

"Oh, yes indeed," replied Merrie. "How else will we know where we're supposed to be at any given time?"

"All right then," said Eleanor. "But hold on a minute." Then she wriggled furiously in the bed, yanking the sheets out of all their tucked-in places and making the bed messy and herself comfortable, which was just the way she liked it.

Merrie put her glasses on her nose and, with a satisfied sigh, opened the laptop.

"Now, let's see," she murmured as a calendar opened on the screen. "Tomorrow is the nineteenth of June, is it not? Aha! Here we are! Oh ho! Can you believe it, my love, I'd almost forgotten that we're traveling to London tomorrow."

Eleanor was pretty certain that Merrie hadn't "almost forgotten" anything.

Merrie tapped at the keypad and muttered as she typed. "Must speak to Hobbs about transporting your you-know-what to the palace tomorrow." She looked up at the princess and smiled broadly. "Oh, won't it be lovely to have him always close by, Your Highness?"

The princess nodded and smiled back, but a tiny frown furrowed her brow. "Merrie? You haven't forgotten that you said I could travel in the helicopter with my parents tomorrow, have you?"

"Of course I haven't," replied Merrie. "You were promised, and as I always say, a promise is a promise." Merrie cleared her throat. "Let's get on, shall we?" Then Merrie began to read the endless list of the things they had to do the next day, but Eleanor stopped listening. She knew from experience that Merrie would remind her about everything ten minutes before it was going to happen anyway, so it wasn't as if she had to memorize anything. Her thoughts drifted down to the last stall in the stables, and she wondered if the unicorn was asleep yet and if he was happy in his new home.

"And at eight oh five precisely, teeth, bed, and

diary. Lights out at eight thirty." Merrie shut the laptop with a snap. "That's everything then. We must be up bright and early so you'll have time to check on your friend before we leave. Now, go straight to sleep." She leaned forward and switched off the bedside light. "Good night, Your Highness," she said, standing in the open bedroom door.

"Merrie?" Eleanor plucked at the coverlet. "Do you think you could ask my parents to come and say—?"

"Oh, dear me, no," said Merrie, shaking her coppery head. "They're far too busy. They're having dinner with the queen of the Netherlands. Adults only. Those Swedes are such sticklers for protocol."

Merrie closed the door, leaving Eleanor alone in the dark. She stared up at the shadowy ceiling. She knew her parents were busy people, but couldn't they once, just once, come and wish her good night?

Chapter 10

SECURITY

Joyce was halfway across the meadow when a warm wind began to blow. The sky was very dark now. The stars had disappeared behind low clouds and it felt like it was about to rain. Joyce tried to fly faster, but the wind was against her.

She was almost at the castle when the storm broke. It was a violent one, with thunder so loud that it threatened to crush her resolve and send her scurrying back to Swinley Hope, but she knew she had to carry on. FLASH! The lightning lit up the entire country-side, showing Joyce how terrifyingly big this world outside the forest really was. Each drop of rain that hit her wings felt like a bowling ball being dropped on them. She knew that once her wings were soaked, it would be impossible to fly. If she could just make it to the castle roof. She struggled on into the wind until at last she was directly over the castle, then she let herself glide as best she could toward the roof.

The tiles were slick with rain, and the second she landed she found herself skidding down the steep roof into a gutter full of rainwater. With an immense effort she pulled herself out, then sat on the edge shivering, trying to think what to do next. She knew she couldn't carry on right away. Even if her wings hadn't been soaked through, she didn't have the strength. She was shattered after such a long flight. Perhaps if she took a little rest, she'd feel better. But her wings would never dry if she slept in the rain. She looked around and saw a warped roof tile a little way along the gutter and thought she might be able to fit beneath it. She could. Almost. Her feet would stick out, but there was nowhere else. It would have to do. She squeezed herself in as best she could, and despite the smell of mold and damp, she curled up and fell fast asleep.

Not far from where Joyce lay, in a small, dark room in the castle, two uniformed security men sat in front of a wall full of video monitors. Unlike the Royal staterooms in the palace, this room was not lavishly decorated. It was in what is known as "below stairs," or the servants' quarters, and it hummed with the expensive thrum of up-to-the-minute technology. Static crackled in the air and accompanied the constant drone of the equipment's cooling fans. These sounds mingled discordantly with the rustle of a cheese and onion potato chip packet that one of the security men was trying to open.

The monitors showed many different images of the Royal estate, which were sent as live feeds from security cameras all over the castle. There on the screen were the main courtyard (seen from three angles), the ballroom, the roofs, the grand dining room, the kitchens, and the great library. One monitor showed the interior of the stables, another the chapel, and another the Royal bedrooms that were on display during the day. There were so many cameras placed around the large castle that each monitor showed at least five images in rotation one after the other.

One of the security guards stared at the monitors with a glazed expression while he munched on the chips and drank hot tea from a plastic cup. The other man was reading the tabloid newspaper the *Daily Stun*, occasionally laughing or grunting at something he read.

A monitor in the fifth row changed its image to show one corner of the roof. There was the warped tile where Joyce lay asleep. Her feet could clearly be seen sticking out of the shadows, but the security guard who was keeping watch did not react. This was because he couldn't actually see her (she being a fairy and him being a non-fairy-seeing human), but the security guard wasn't the only one who was watching the monitors. Other, keener eyes were watching, too.

High up in the corner of the room, where the wall met the ceiling, there was a horizontal crack in the plaster and beyond this crack another security room. This room was much smaller than the first, but it was infinitely better run. Castle fairies, you see, are renowned for their efficiency. They are masters of getting things done, as long as what they are doing helps the Royal Family.

The castle fairies loved the Royal Family a great deal and considered it a great privilege to serve them. They had even set up their own security room, just in case the human guards weren't doing their job properly. No fewer than five small telescopes on tripods stood in the fairy security room, each with its business end poking through the crack in the corner and pointing at the bank of monitors.

On this night, as on most nights, William Butler,

the fairy in charge of the fairy part of the castle—the fairy equivalent of the human butler in the Royal household—was staring intently through one of the telescopes. Unlike the other fairies, he was not watching the images on the monitors. He was busy looking over the guard's shoulder and reading the newspaper. William Butler liked to keep abreast of what was happening in the world, and, more importantly, he felt it was his duty to see that there had been no more leaks to the newspapers.

It was a troubled time for William Butler. Leaks had been springing up everywhere recently. Every day there were new reports in the papers divulging more and more details about the private lives of the Royal Family. It was ridiculous, but people seemed to find even the smallest details about them fascinating. Apparently they enjoyed reading about how the queen had lilac bedsheets and how the king liked his eggs scrambled, not poached, as had previously been thought. And when the papers got wind of the fact that, horror of horrors, Princess Eleanor actually liked ketchup on her eggs (and not good English ketchup, but some imported American brand), there was a national outcry. The princess was even accused of being unpatriotic, which had led to questions being asked in the House of Commons.

"Oh, for heaven's sakes!" groaned William Butler in dismay. "Just listen to this: 'Our sources tell us that Princess Eleanor gives her pony, Lemon, carrots rolled in brown sugar on a daily basis,' and they claim that that's why the pony is such a tub." William Butler shook his head. "I'd like to get my hands on whoever is leaking this nonsense. Some spy at the palace, some dirty little mole. I think—"

"Sir, sir," cried a fairy named Bosley, who was manning telescope number three. "I've got something on seventeen. Could be an intruder, sir."

Butler stared hard through his telescope and then drew a sharp breath.

"You're right, man. Well done." He picked up a telephone and punched in a number. "Thrivens!" he shouted into the mouthpiece. "Sound the alarm. There's an unknown pair of legs sticking out of the shadows on the roof. Get a patrol unit over to the upper northwest quadrant ASAP. What? Yes, I said legs. L-E-G-S. Legs. No, I do not know to whom they belong. Stop asking questions and check it out pronto."

Poor Joyce. It was a terrible shock to wake up to find twelve bayonets pointing right at her. The twelve bayonets belonged to twelve of the very first nonforest fairies she'd ever met. It was a shock. She didn't get a chance to say anything before two burly fairy guards grabbed her, pulled her to her feet, and held her fast.

"What am I supposed to have done?" she asked tremulously.

Commander Thrivens, head of security operations at the castle, shot her a ferocious look. "We'll be asking the questions," he said. "Come along nice and quiet. We're not going to hurt you"—he raised an eyebrow—"much."

Moments later the guards set her on the turret roof and marched her across the tiles and through a door. Once inside, they quickly led her down one long corridor, then up another until they reached a door. Here they stopped, knocked, and, when told to enter, opened the door and pushed her through.

The room in which Joyce now found herself reminded her, in a bad way, of her headmistress's study at school. It was a bland office. A functional room devoid of warmth or decoration. There were no pictures on the rough stone walls, the carpet was gray and worn, and the little furniture there was—one large wooden desk, five chairs (all hard), a bank of bashed-up metal filing cabinets, and a single dead plant in a chipped pot—did little to cheer the grim setting.

William Butler stood beside one of the chairs and

stared piercingly at Joyce as she was brought in. He instructed the guards to sit her in the chair.

"Mr. Butler," growled the commander as he loomed over Joyce, "would you like me to begin the torture now, sir?"

Joyce's knees trembled. Torture?

"Thank you, Thrivens, I'll take care of this," replied William Butler. "Send Daphne in on your way out, would you?" The commander saluted, then he and his men left the room. A moment later there was a soft knock at the door.

"Ah, good. Come in, Daphne," called William Butler as a tall fairy with beautiful violet wings entered, carrying a pencil and notebook.

"Sit over there," said Mr. Butler, pointing to a chair. "And make sure you get every word. No detail is too small in a case as serious as this."

Daphne glanced at Joyce and their eyes met briefly. She doesn't look much older than me, thought Joyce. She dared a tiny smile, but the fairy didn't return it. She went directly to the chair, sat down, crossed one leg over the other, balanced her notebook on her knee, and waited with her pencil poised above the paper like a viper waiting to strike.

Mr. Butler stood with his back to the fireplace. He

lowered his head and stared at Joyce from beneath his bushy eyebrows.

"You're not going to hurt me, are you?" asked Joyce in a very small voice.

William Butler looked surprised. "Hurt you?" he asked gruffly. "Of course we're not going to hurt you!" he said, clasping his hands behind his back and rocking on his heels. "Now, why were you trespassing on the roof?"

Joyce told him everything that had happened and Daphne scribbled away, getting it all down in her notebook. Joyce had just mentioned how the unicorn had been taken out of the forest when Mr. Butler interrupted.

"I must stop you there," he said. "Let me see if I have this right. You came here to find the unicorn and take him back to your forest. Is that correct?"

Joyce nodded.

"Aha! It appears you are unaware of one important fact." Mr. Butler paused. "You see, the 'big people,' or 'humans,' who live in this castle are not ordinary ones. They are royalty; i.e., they are members of the Royal Family and this is their home.

"Swinley Castle and the entire estate belong to Their Majesties the king and queen of England. By law everything in Swinley Forest, every bird, deer, tree, flower, *and unicorn,* belongs to them. It's an ancient and unbreakable law."

Joyce fought back the tears as she tried to explain. "But if . . . ," she said bravely, "if you don't let me take the unicorn back, the forest will die and all my family and all the fairies will have to leave."

William Butler shook his head. "Oh, I don't think so," he said. "All that guff about a forest not being able to survive without its unicorn, that's just superstitious twaddle. You and the other forest fairies will be fine. You'll see. You can stay here until the rain's stopped, and then I'll have my guards escort you home. Daphne?"

Without looking at Joyce, the note-taking fairy stood up and headed out the door. William Butler followed her, patting Joyce's shoulder as he passed. "Get some rest," he said. "And don't look so worried. Everything will be fine." Then he shut the door behind him.

"No, you're wrong!" Joyce jumped up to go after him but the door was locked. "No!" she cried, hammering on the wood. "You're so wrong! The forest *will* die without the unicorn, and the unicorn will suffer as well." Then, feeling absolutely hopeless, she went back to the chair, covered her face with her hands, and wept until, a few minutes later, a soft knock made her look up. She heard a key turn in the lock, and then the door opened. To Joyce's surprise, Daphne came back in carefully carrying a little mug.

"I brought you some cocoa," she said with a big, friendly smile. Joyce was so astonished she just stared at her.

"It's all right," laughed Daphne, setting the mug on the desk. "I'm not horrible really, that was just an act." She glanced about and then moved closer to Joyce and whispered conspiratorially. "I didn't want Mr. Butler to think I was in the least bit interested in your story. I didn't want him suspecting that I wanted to help you recover your unicorn."

"H-help me?" stammered Joyce, not believing what she was hearing. "You want to help me?"

"Yes, I do," replied Daphne. "Mr. Butler's not a bad fairy, but he's such a stickler for the letter of the law, he gets blinded by it. He can't see that this is a special case. And trust me, there's no reasoning with him. He won't change his mind. But don't worry, where there's a will there's a way. Now, I think it'd be best if you stay here while I look for your unicorn. I'll come and get you as soon as I've found him. Shouldn't take me long. Drink your cocoa while it's hot. Back soon." Then, with another flash of her bright smile, she was gone.

It was late. The clock on the desk said it was five to three in the morning. Joyce was exhausted. Just a little nap, she thought as she folded her arms on the desk, laid her head on them, and closed her eyes. Within seconds she was sound asleep.

"Come on, sleepyhead, wake up," said a voice in Joyce's ear.

Joyce woke with a jolt. The clock said it was almost five thirty. Daphne stood by the door. "Did you find . . . ?" Joyce asked.

"Yes." Daphne nodded. "He's safe in the stables, but we need to get him out of here before the rest of the castle wakes up. I'll tell you why on the way. Come on. Follow me."

They ran quickly along the corridor, hiding once or twice in doorways to avoid being spotted by the fairy guards, then down a narrow spiral staircase that eventually led them to an outside door. Daphne opened it.

"Through here," Daphne said as she ushered Joyce outside.

Dawn comes extremely early in England in the summertime, and by five forty-five the sun had already been up an hour. The previous night's rain had cleared the air and in the early morning stillness the world looked newly washed and beautiful. It felt good to be outside.

"That's the stables," said Daphne, pointing across the cobbled courtyard to a large brick building. It looked miles away.

"This is where we've got to be really careful," whispered Daphne. "The humans have security cameras everywhere. That's how you got caught before. Fairy guards watch the monitors twenty-four/seven, and we do not want to get caught. We have to fly when those cameras are turned away. We'll take it in stages. First to the water trough. Okay. Fly only on my signal. Ready?" Joyce nodded nervously. Daphne waited, intently watching the cameras on the roof. "Not yet . . . Not yet . . . Now!" she commanded, and Joyce found herself flying at breakneck speed a few inches above the cobbles.

When they reached the water trough, Joyce saw there was nowhere to hide between there and the stable entrance. How on earth would they avoid the cameras now?

"Give it a minute," said Daphne. "There!" Joyce looked and saw the first of several large black cars pull into the courtyard. "Just what I'd been hoping for," said Daphne. "The Royal Family is returning to London today. Pretty soon this courtyard will be full of cars and humans, which means we'll be able to hide from the cameras and the guards, but watch yourself, you don't want to get crushed or run over!"

As she flew across the courtyard beside Daphne, Joyce was scared out of her wits. The cars were terrifyingly big and there seemed to be no end of them. They glided by on their monstrous wheels, often coming dangerously close to the two fairies. At first Joyce was horrified when Daphne flew right under the cars, but she soon realized that was the safest course. There they couldn't be trod on or squished under one of the heavy suitcases or boxes that were being stacked in piles before being loaded into the cars.

Joyce didn't know how they did it, but eventually they landed and collapsed, breathless, just inside the stable door.

"Never . . . huh . . . thought . . . we'd make it . . . ," Daphne panted; then she glanced back through the open door, her eyes scanning the sky. "It doesn't look like anyone's after us," she said. "They probably don't even know you're missing yet. Come on, your unicorn is in the last stall on the left. Stay close behind me and keep against the wall. There aren't too many cameras in here, so there are plenty of blind spots. Let's go."

Joyce flew after Daphne as she zigzagged down the stables. They traveled fast and soon reached the last stall with its cloth-covered railings. Daphne veered up and landed on the horizontal bar at the top of the railings. A second later Joyce alighted beside her and looked into the stall. The unicorn and the yellow pony were standing by the hay bin calmly munching their breakfast.

Joyce was thankful and relieved when she saw the unicorn; thankful because it hadn't really been so very difficult to find him, and relieved because he looked exactly the same as when she'd last seen him. She'd been worried that having been out of the forest for so many hours could have affected his health, but the sheen of his coat seemed just as glossy, his eyes were still bright, his golden horn and hooves still shone, and his mane and tail still sparkled.

"So there he is," said Daphne. "But how do we get him out of here? Now, let's think this through. There's a door at the far end of the stables that leads onto the back road, and that should be quiet about now. So far, so good. Then a few hundred yards along that road you'll find a small iron gate in the castle wall. Go through that and you're in the meadow—almost home. But of course there are a couple of problems." She counted them off on her fingers. "One: how do we get him out of the stall? Two: how do we sneak him past that groom out there who seems to be keeping

90

watch, and three: how do we get him down the back road and through the gate without any of the fairy guards spotting us? Hmmm. . . . Difficult, but not impossible."

"Not impossible, but very definitely ILLEGAL!" boomed an angry voice behind them. Startled, Joyce and Daphne spun around to find a furious William Butler and an entire squadron of fairy guards hovering in the air behind them.

"Attempting to steal the property of the crown is a very serious crime! Arrest them!" he barked. Two guards swiftly landed on the rail, caught hold of Joyce's arms, and held her fast. Two more grabbed Daphne.

William Butler frowned at her. "Daphne, Daphne, Daphne," he sighed with a shake of his head. "And I thought you were doing so well as my secretary. I thought the added responsibility had stopped you from interfering with castle affairs. I am exceedingly disappointed."

"But, Dad—" Daphne began.

"He's your father?" Joyce said, but Daphne wasn't listening.

"Dad, you can't let Princess Eleanor take the unicorn to—"

"Yes, I can," retorted Mr. Butler. "The law is the

law. Her Highness has every right to take the unicorn to London with the rest of her belongings." Daphne opened her mouth to say something, but her father stopped her. "We will talk about this later. Guards, take them and lock them both up somewhere until the entire Royal household has left," he said. "After that, you can take that one"—he pointed angrily at Joyce—"back to the forest and send my daughter to me."

"Very good, sir," said the captain, saluting. At his command the squadron rose into the dusty air and flew swiftly toward the roof. Two guards carried Joyce as though she weighed no more than a piece of tissue. She kept her eyes on the unicorn below in the stall and willed herself not to cry.

It didn't matter what William Butler said about the law. The law was wrong. The unicorn had to return to the forest. Joyce wiped her nose on her shoulder and made up her mind. However far away this London was, she would go there and find the unicorn and somehow she would bring him back. She would not go home without him.

The fairy squadron banked to their left, flew swiftly through an open skylight, and shot out into the summer sky.

Chapter 11

THE MAP

As the guards flew Joyce over the crowded court-yard toward the main building, she noticed a strange machine parked on one of the castle's flat roofs. The body of the machine was black and shiny like a bee-tle's carapace, and there was a gold coat of arms on one of its doors. Two long blades that crossed over one an-other and formed an X were fixed to the top. These blades began to turn, slowly at first, but they soon picked up speed, spinning faster and faster until they were moving so quickly they were just a blur.

A strip of red carpet stretched from the machine to a modern glass door in the castle wall. The door opened and a well-dressed couple came out and hurried along the red carpet, crouching slightly as they drew near to the machine. Once they'd climbed in, the black shiny doors were closed and moments later the machine lifted into the air and sped into the distance.

"What was that?" asked Joyce, amazed.

"That's an helicopter," said the guard beside her. "Humans can't fly like us, see, so they have machines to carry 'em about."

"Quiet back there!" shouted Mr. Butler. "Don't fraternize with the prisoner, Corporal Baker!"

"Sorry," Joyce whispered to the guard.

Corporal Baker winked at her and put a finger to his lips.

Joyce looked down at the roof where the helicopter had been and saw a blond-haired girl burst through the door. She watched as the girl ran down the red carpet, then stopped and stared at the rapidly diminishing helicopter in the sky.

Joyce knew immediately it was the princess. A moment later the massive man who'd been with the girl in the forest came through the door. He ran with one finger to his ear, and as he ran, he swiftly scrutinized the rooftops. The glass door opened again and the bony woman with the coppery hair scuttled out and scurried along the red carpet to the princess.

The two gray-suited fairies were there, too. They were flying in wide circles above the humans. They shot down and landed on the big man's shoulders as another black helicopter came in to land on the roof. The man stepped forward and put himself between the princess and the machine.

Once the helicopter had landed the blades slowed, but they didn't stop spinning completely. The big man ran to the machine, opened the door for the princess and the bony woman to get in, and climbed in after them with the two fairies still on his shoulders. The blades sped up, and soon this second helicopter lifted off the roof and flew into the distance.

Inside the second Royal helicopter the princess and her governess sat in the rear seats while Captain Simperington sat up front beside the pilot. The princess stared out of the window. She was disappointed not to be flying in the first helicopter with her parents.

"I know I promised, my sweet, but you know why I couldn't let you go with them, don't you, my darling?" asked Merrie in a tremulous voice. "You are the sole heir to the throne and it would be disastrous if you were with your parents and something horrible happened to the helicopter that was carrying all of"—Merrie pulled out her handkerchief and dabbed it against her eyes—"all of you . . . together."

"It's all right," said Eleanor. "Merrie, please . . . don't get upset. I understand, really I do."

Merrie sniffed and dried her eyes. She took a pocket mirror out of her purse and made sure her tears hadn't smudged her makeup. Just as she was replacing the mirror, the helicopter took off. Princess Eleanor gazed down at the castle as it grew smaller.

"Oh, goody!" Merrie exclaimed a little too cheerily. "We're on our way properly now, aren't we, Your Highness?"

The helicopter banked to the east as it flew over the castle. "Wheeeeeeeee," chuckled Merrie like a kid on a rollercoaster.

Eleanor always cringed when Merrie laughed like that. It wasn't so much because that particular laugh of Merrie's sounded like a machine gun rat-at-at-ating, nor because when she laughed like that Merrie opened her mouth so wide that she showed all her fillings. No, Eleanor disliked this particular laugh because it was a fake laugh. Merrie only ever laughed this way when she was trying to be the princess's best friend.

Princess Eleanor watched the ground whiz by below. What would it be like to be able to fly? she wondered. That tiny creature she'd seen yesterday could fly. She tried to see her again in her mind's eye. It wasn't the first time she'd seen something like that.

She had a vague memory from a long time ago. She was perhaps three or four years old and she'd been lying in bed, idly gazing at the chandelier, when she'd seen two such winged creatures, little flying women, wearing black maids' uniforms with little white aprons. They were dusting the tear-shaped crystals on the chandelier with feather dusters and making them twist and sparkle. Eleanor had watched them for ages until, when they'd finished their work, they'd flown all the way to the cornice and disappeared behind an elaborate plaster swirl.

And there'd been another time, too—in the grand banquet hall at the palace. She had gone in to look for her parents. They weren't there, but as she was leaving she noticed something odd on the table. She'd crept closer and seen a tiny man polishing the crystal sherry glasses with a little yellow cloth. He was wearing a footman's uniform—a green coat and black knickerbockers—and whistling as he worked. She remembered trying to get a closer look, but then Merrie had burst in and scared the little man away.

These incidents had happened so long ago that the princess had come to believe that she had just imagined them or dreamed them up. But what if she hadn't? Was it possible that they were actually fairies? And that tiny girl in the forest? Was she one, too? Did fairies exist? Eleanor thought about it. If unicorns were real, wasn't there a chance that fairies might be, too? But if that was true, there had to be more than four of them in the world. Why couldn't she see them all the time?

Perhaps seeing fairies takes practice, she thought. Maybe if I work at it, I'll be able to see more of them. With that in mind, the princess spent the rest of the helicopter flight staring intently at the summer sky looking for fairies.

The cell into which Joyce and Daphne were thrown wasn't really a cell at all. It was a linen cupboard where the castle fairies kept their clean linens, and it smelled, rather pleasantly, of fresh laundry. They weren't really thrown into it, either. The guards were kind and polite.

"Sorry about this, Daphne," said the captain of the guard. "But you know your father. I'll have to lock you in, but it shouldn't be for long. The Royal household will be out of here within the hour if we're lucky."

"Thanks," said Daphne. The captain went out, and they heard the key turn in the lock.

"Joyce?" said Daphne. "I'm sorry it didn't work out. My dad isn't really that bad, it's just that he believes absolutely in the law, even when the law makes no sense. Maybe when you get back to the forest you can tell your alders that—"

Joyce shook her head. "I can't go back to the forest," she said. "Not without the unicorn."

Daphne looked surprised. "But they're taking him to the palace. That's in London. It's miles away."

"It doesn't matter how far it is," replied Joyce, hoping she sounded more confident than she actually felt. "I have to bring him back."

Daphne burst out laughing. "Good for you, Joyce. It's quite a journey. You'll need some supplies. Wait here."

"But the door's locked—" Joyce stopped as Daphne stuck her arm under a pile of sheets, felt around, and then pulled out a key.

"I'm always getting in trouble and sent in here," she giggled, unlocking the door. "So one day I came and hid a spare key up here for emergencies. Be back in a mo."

Daphne was not gone very long. When she returned, her face was flushed and she was smiling. She put a small package and a bottle on a shelf, then pulled a rectangle of folded paper out of her waistband.

"I brought you a map," she said, carefully unfolding the paper. "I'm afraid it's pretty old, but things change so slowly in England that most of the landmarks from here to London will be the same."

Joyce looked at the map. It was dotted with tiny, hand-painted pictures of houses, churches, castles, forests, and lakes. Each picture had a name written beside it in neat cursive script—names like *Bodlington* or *Swintern* or *Lower Bottom*. The pictures were connected to one another by squiggly lines that reminded Joyce of the veins on a leaf.

"This'll show you the way to London," said Daphne. "Do you see?"

Joyce shook her head. "I hadn't even heard of London until today," she admitted.

"That's all right," said Daphne kindly. "Look. We're here at Swinley Castle." She pointed to the painting of a castle on the far left of the map. "And the Royal Family have gone to their palace in London, which is there." She tapped the picture of a white tower with four turrets surrounded by a cluster of buildings. "So if you fly from one landmark—"

"—to the next, I'll be able to find my way there," exclaimed Joyce, suddenly understanding.

"Exactly," replied Daphne.

"And that's the palace?" Joyce asked, pointing to the white tower.

Daphne laughed. "No, that's the Tower of London. Buckingham Palace wouldn't have been built when this map was made. But don't worry, once you get to London you'll find the palace easily. It's by far the most famous place there."

Joyce put her index finger on the forest and her middle finger on the castle, and then, keeping her fingers the same distance apart, she walked them from the castle to the palace. It took thirty-four steps for her fingers to reach London, which meant that it was thirty-four times as far from the castle to the palace as it had been from the forest to the castle.

"It's such a long way," she said, dismayed.

"You don't have to fly it all at once," said Daphne with an encouraging smile. "Break the journey into smaller sections and you'll get there in the end."

But what little confidence Joyce had was waning fast. Now she saw nothing but problems piling up. She felt close to tears again. "Even if I make it all the way there, and even if I find the unicorn, how on earth will I get him back here? It's not like I'm just making him run across the meadow and up to the trees, is it?"

Daphne shook her head. "I don't know exactly

how you'll manage it, but you'll find a way. Sometimes you just have to trust that things will work out." Joyce smiled. It was just the sort of thing Sam would say.

She folded up the map. "I guess I'd better get started, then," she said.

"That's the spirit," cheered Daphne, picking up the package and the bottle and handing them to Joyce. "Take these. There are sandwiches for the journey, and water, too. You can keep the map. There are plenty more in a castle as old as this. Come on."

Joyce thanked her and put them carefully in Sam's canvas bag.

Out on the roof Joyce blinked in the sunshine. Shading her eyes, she looked across the meadow at the forest on the hill. She noticed that the trees looked different. It was too early in the summer for the leaves to turn, but their color seemed to have faded. Was this because the unicorn was not there?

Joyce unfolded the map, studied it, and then refolded it so that the section with the castle on it was visible.

"You know where you're going?" asked Daphne.

"Yes, here," replied Joyce, pointing to a town marked on the map. "It's called Wheatby. I want to make it there before evening." She folded the map and put it away in the pocket of the knapsack.

Daphne smiled encouragingly. "Sounds good," she said, giving Joyce a big hug. "Fly safe."

"Thanks," said Joyce. "I hope you don't get in trouble with your dad for helping me."

"Probably will." Daphne shrugged. "But then, I'm always in trouble, so it won't be *that* much of a change."

"Thanks again," called Joyce as she took off. Once airborne, she turned east and was soon sailing high on the warm summer breeze, leaving Swinley Castle and the forest far behind her.

Chapter 12

WHEATBY

It takes less than twenty minutes for a Royal helicopter to fly from Swinley Castle to Buckingham Palace. It takes a lot longer for a horse van traveling on the eternally busy roads into London. By the time Hobbs was reversing the horse van containing Lemon and the unicorn up the main aisle of the stables at Buckingham Palace, the princess had been home for over two hours.

She could hardly wait to see her unicorn. She wanted to make sure that he was comfortable, that he and Lemon were getting along, and that the journey hadn't been too taxing for him.

Merrie had endeavored to distract the princess with schoolwork, but her usually exemplary pupil was finding it nearly impossible to concentrate on her lessons.

When, finally, word came that Hobbs had arrived, Merrie instructed the princess to close her schoolbooks and then, on the understanding that she would resume her studies later, allowed her to go to the stables to see her unicorn.

Once again Hobbs had housed Lemon and the unicorn in a stall at the farthest and least-used end of the stables, far away from prying eyes. Once again he had covered the bars with sacking so no one would accidentally see anything they weren't supposed to.

When she got to the stables, the princess ran the entire length of the building. Captain Simperington trotted close behind, while Merrie huffed and puffed a long way back.

The princess was already in the stall by the time Merrie caught up with her. As promised, she'd brought sugar carrots for her unicorn and her pony. Both animals ate them with relish and bothered her for more.

Merrie allowed the princess to stay for a full hour before insisting it was time for afternoon lessons to begin.

Joyce flew high above the pleasantly rolling countryside that lies to the east of Swinley Castle. The sky was a clear, clear blue. Joyce could barely believe what was happening to her. Three days ago she'd never even seen the sky as a whole. Now she was seeing a world she could never have imagined.

The landscapes were fascinating and new to her. The fields, the hedgerows, the copses, the houses big and small, the gray roads, and all the strange new vehicles she saw on them all kept her spellbound for hours.

I can't believe that no one at home cares about any of this! she thought. She looked up in the sky and saw something far above her. It was white with stiff wings that stuck out at the sides and gleamed in the sun. A line of white vapor trailed behind it. Joyce laughed. "I have no idea what you are!" she shouted at the top of her voice. "But whatever you are, you're amazing!"

With the map to guide her, the trip wasn't as difficult as she'd feared. She made excellent progress, and by late afternoon she'd passed the old tithe barn and the ruined Laistran Castle and could see a sprawling town in the far distance. That has to be Wheatby, she thought, pleased she would make it there before dark. Joyce flapped her wings and, having found her rhythm, cut effortlessly through the air.

That afternoon the princess sat at her desk, studying algebra from a textbook, but her thoughts were only half on her equations. She couldn't help daydreaming just a little. There was the unicorn to think about, and the possibility that fairies might actually be real. She was staring up at the chandelier, hoping to see fairy maids or footmen cleaning it, when Merrie's "ahem" reminded her that she was supposed to be studying.

Merrie sat across the room at her small desk, her laptop open before her. She was hard at work. She'd offered to research unicorns online for the princess.

"If we want your unicorn to be happy here," Merrie had whispered earnestly on the way back from the stables, "we must arm ourselves to the teeth with information. We'll need to know how best to take care of him, how to feed him, and how to make him feel at home. If you like, my Princess Baby, I could have a poke about on the Internet for you."

Princess Eleanor had readily agreed. Looking over at her governess now, focused so intently on her computer screen, the princess was impressed. It was incredible that Merrie, who hated all things horsey, seemed to love the unicorn almost as much as she did herself. It looked like the governess was enjoying herself with the research because she kept chuckling quietly and making notes. The princess couldn't wait to hear what she'd discovered.

The princess was right. Merrie was enjoying herself. She loved the Internet. It was just so useful. Within moments of typing the words "unicorns" and "real" in the search box, she had found, amongst the multitude of advertisements for unicorn posters, jewelry, and bed linen, the Web site of an American organization called the J. J. Rosenthal Institute.

According to their home page, the J. J. Rosenthal Institute was an independent foundation "dedicated to the academic pursuit of all things paranormal." These words also crowned the upper curve of their logo—a white circle with a dark blue eye in the center. Their mission statement proclaimed that their "ultimate goal is the discoveryfication, authentification, and verification of all creatures of mythical significance."

As Merrie poked about on the site, she soon discovered that the billionaire benefactor and founder of the institute, J. J. Rosenthal himself, was offering a reward of one million dollars to anyone who could provide irrefutable proof that any creature of "mythical significance" actually and undeniably existed. It was gratifying to find that unicorns were at the top of the Institute's "most wanted" list.

"May I go back to the stables now, Merrie?" asked the princess.

Merrie looked up and grinned. "Yes, of course you may, my love. Enjoy!"

The sunset that evening was a stunner. Joyce kept glancing back at it as she flew. Red and pink and dove-gray clouds spread across the sky. Golden shafts of light shot out from behind them and set the edges of the clouds on fire.

The landscape changed as she neared the town. At first there were just one or two houses on a hillside, but soon there were a few more and then more until there were houses and buildings everywhere. Joyce checked the map. This was definitely Wheatby. Now all she had to do was to head toward Millets Mountain, the next landmark on her map.

She flew over streets and streets of big people houses set out in neat lines with narrow paths between them and patches of green behind. As she neared the center of the town, the roads became wider, with large leafy trees growing along either side. The houses were bigger here, and many had large gardens with fountains and swimming pools.

The smell of meat being barbequed on grills

wafted up into the evening air, making Joyce realize how hungry she was. She'd eaten all Daphne's sandwiches hours ago when she'd stopped briefly at Laistran Castle, and now she had nothing for supper. She tried not to think about that and attempted to distract herself by watching Wheatby's fairies.

It worked. There were plenty to watch. Joyce had never seen so many fairies all at once, not even on the busiest market days in Swinley Hope, and she forgot all about her rumbling stomach as she gazed about her. There were fairies everywhere in Wheatby. They were flying in the air, gathering in the trees, or walking in groups along the edges of the rooftops.

Joyce peered at them. Like the fairies she'd seen at the castle, all these had beautiful, strong-looking wings and they knew how to use them—that alone made them different from the forest fairies back home. The clothes they wore fascinated her. In the forest there was a strict code. Forest fairies dressed in shades of either green or brown, depending on the season, but here the Wheatby fairies were wearing bright colors, as though it didn't matter if they stood out. They wore their hair in all sorts of styles, too, and some of them had painted faces, which startled her at first. For the most part they didn't look *that* unlike the fairies in Swinley Hope, even though some she passed had different-colored skin and spoke in languages she couldn't understand.

She flew over a park and saw fairy children playing hopscotch on the top of the climbing frame and fairy families picnicking by a pond, their suppers set out on leaves.

The buildings beneath her changed again. Some were huge with flat roofs and no gardens. Others were three, four, even five stories high with lots of windows. There was one pretty building with white walls and a thatched roof. Its gardens were crowded with big people sitting at tables, chatting and laughing. It reminded her of the Twisted Elm, the pub in the market square back home.

She flew up to the roof of the tallest building and checked her map again. Wheatby and Millets Mountain looked quite far apart on the map and there were no landmarks painted in between. Joyce scanned the horizon. It shouldn't have been too hard to spot a mountain, but by now the sun had set and the sky in the east was already dark. She couldn't see any mountains at all.

Perhaps, she thought, she could ask a local fairy for directions. With this in mind, she flew across the roof and looked over the edge of the tall building. On the other side there was a broad street lined with shops.

Baskets full of blooming flowers hung from every lamppost and lines of bunting criss-crossed the street, the colored cloth triangles fluttering in the breeze. There were no cars or vans on this road, just lots of big people walking leisurely along, gazing in the shop windows or meandering down the middle of the street.

There were plenty of fairies out for an evening stroll, too. They were walking along the roofs of the shops, strolling in little groups, chatting as they went. Joyce plucked up her courage. Maybe one of them would be able to help her.

She quickly raked her fingers through her hair, rubbed her face with her hands, and then, hoping she didn't look a total fright, flew down and landed on a shop roof. The first person she approached was a kind-looking older lady fairy who was walking three small fairy-sized dogs on red leashes. This fairy was talking to the dogs in such a sweet manner that Joyce was sure she'd help her.

"Excuse me," she began, but when the old lady fairy lifted her head she looked Joyce up and down with cold, silvery eyes and the three little dogs snarled and yapped. Joyce backed away.

"Riffraff!" muttered the old fairy as she hurried her dogs away. "I don't know what this town is coming to."

Joyce noticed other fairies were looking at her

askance. She wondered what she had done wrong. She'd only been asking for help. She'd said "excuse me." She hadn't been rude. Why was everyone looking at her like that?

She tried asking a younger female fairy, but she didn't even stop. She just glided on by as though Joyce wasn't even there.

She would have to try again. Joyce steeled herself and approached a family who were sauntering down the street.

"Excuse me . . . ," she said, smiling.

The mother fairy stopped and glared at her.

"Shoo!" she said, waggling her long white fingers at Joyce. "Out of the way."

This response was so rude that instead of making Joyce run away it made her determined not to give up. Mustering all her courage, she held the map out for the fairy to see. "I was wondering if you cou—"

The white-fingered fairy suddenly rapped Joyce's knuckles with her folded fan.

"Move away," she warned Joyce. "Now! Or I shall have you arrested!"

"I—I—I—I—" was all Joyce could manage to say, because just at that moment she saw a uniformed police officer heading in her direction. He was the biggest fairy she'd ever seen and he looked very cross.

"Ah, good, Constable Wickham," said the white-fingered fairy when she saw the officer. "Over here, quick as you can."

Joyce desperately wanted to fly away, but she suspected that would only make things worse. The policeman had huge wings and could probably outfly her easily. She would just have to explain that she'd only been asking for directions. She couldn't be arrested for that, could she?

"I believe, Constable Wickham," said the white-fingered fairy in a snotty voice, "it was agreed at the last council meeting that any itinerants, undesirables, or riffraff were to be removed from our streets and no longer allowed to loiter about upsetting our children or spoiling the view. Am I not correct?"

"That's right, Mrs. Fothergill," replied the constable.

"Then what is this . . . this . . . person doing here, accosting innocent townsfolk and preventing them from enjoying their evening stroll?"

"My apologies, Mrs. Fothergill, I'll deal with it forthwith," said the police officer, coldly appraising Joyce.

Joyce tried to show him the map. "I was only asking for directions. I didn't mean any—"

Constable Wickham swiped the map out of

Joyce's hand, roughly folded it up and put it in his breast pocket, and then snapped one half of a pair of handcuffs on her wrist.

"Come along," he commanded, immediately setting off at a run, which forced Joyce to run as well. The policeman flapped his great gray wings and took to the air, pulling her up behind him.

"That's more like it, Constable," called the white-fingered fairy as Joyce and the policeman circled around and flew over the crowd.

"Always glad to be of service, ma'am," shouted Constable Wickham. Then, in a quieter voice, he added, "Always happy to help you trumped-up lot think better of yourselves than you already do."

Joyce stared at the constable in amazement. He smiled back sheepishly.

"Sorry," he said. "But her sort get my goat. They're a horrible lot. They make a ton of money, then move down here and act like they're royalty. I'd leave, but I love this town. I've been here all my life with my family. Oh, but I can't stand them. That lot, I mean, not my family."

They flew by a street lamp and the policeman looked at Joyce properly. "Blimey," he said. "You look half-dead, you poor thing. Hold on to my arm and I'll do the flying for both of us."

"Thanks," she said. "I've traveled a long way today. I wasn't meaning to make trouble. I was just trying to ask for directions. Then I was going to leave, really."

"As far as I'm concerned, you can stay as long as you like. Now then, are you hungry? My missus'll have supper on and you're more than welcome to join us. Aggie always makes more than I ought to eat, hence this," he laughed, slapping his large belly with his free hand. "And Aggie said she'd make me a sticky toffee pudding tonight, if that takes your fancy."

Joyce smiled. Sticky toffee pudding was her favorite. "I'd like that very much, thank you," she said.

"That's settled then," said the constable. "Tell you what—after we've eaten, I'll have a look at your map and see if I can help. Not far to go now. Just a few roofs past that big old factory over there."

Constable Wickham soon banked left, then headed down toward a roof where Joyce could see a pretty little house standing at the base of a terra-cotta chimney pot.

"Here we are," said the constable cheerily as they landed. "Not a palace, but we like it. Now hold out your hand and let's get that handcuff off. There, that's the ticket."

Chapter 13

Egg Salad Sandwiches

The constable's house had the prettiest garden Joyce had ever seen. Vegetables and flowers of all varieties flourished everywhere.

"My Aggie's a magician in the garden," laughed the constable when he saw the look on Joyce's face. "She's spent years cultivating miniature versions of all sorts of human fruits and vegetables. These here are tomatoes, these are runner beans, and those big leafy ones are cabbages, greens, and lettuce. She's a marvel with flowers, too. Look."

Joyce nodded and gazed at the flowers. There

were tiny buttercups, sunflowers, and even bluebells—
all fairy-sized and perfect.

Just then a small, tubby fairy popped up from behind a rhododendron bush.

"Wicky, you're home!" she cried, hurrying across
the garden to give the policeman a kiss. "And you've
brought company," she added, beaming at Joyce.
"How lovely! You're staying for supper, I hope?"

"Please, if that's all right," replied Joyce, liking
Aggie instantly.

"Joyce here was being persecuted by the charming
Fothergills," said Wicky, removing his helmet. "I had
to pretend to arrest her."

"Oh, Wicky, they're getting worse, aren't they?"
said Aggie. Then she smiled again at Joyce. "Ach!
Enough about them. Supper won't be a moment."

"Can I help?" asked Joyce.

"No, no," replied Aggie, heading toward the
house. "Wicky and me will see to everything. You sit
down at the table there. Won't be a tick."

Joyce sat down at the large wooden table in the
garden and looked around. There were so many flowers and plants it was hard to see where the garden
stopped and the house began. A jasmine vine, heavy
with white star-shaped flowers, grew up one side of
the house, and tiny pink roses in full bloom climbed

up the other. The house was a lean-to, which meant that it only had three walls and used the chimney pot as its fourth. More roses grew over its little front door, there were pink geraniums in the boxes beneath the windows, and the walls, where you could see them, were painted white.

"Thought we'd need a little light," said Aggie as she came out carrying a lit candle. She put it on the table, then took knives and forks and napkins from her apron pocket and began to set three places for supper.

Wicky arrived a moment later, holding a tray in one hand like a waiter. He'd changed his clothes and was now wearing a comfortable old shirt and baggy trousers. As he set the dishes on the table, he smiled at her. Wicky had such a kind face that Joyce couldn't believe she'd ever been afraid of him.

Joyce's mouth watered when she saw what there was to eat. It was a feast. There were sausage rolls, tiny vol-au-vents stuffed with creamed mushrooms, a round loaf of freshly baked bread, creamy white butter, and a plate of different cheeses. There were slices of Aggie's tomatoes, a green salad, chopped red beets, some pickled peppers, and best of all a large platter of egg salad sandwiches. For dessert there was a bowl full of Aggie's fairy-sized summer berries and a dish of clotted cream to have with them. But there was no sign of a sticky toffee pudding. Joyce tried not to feel disappointed.

"Help yourself, Joyce," Aggie said cheerily. "Wicky, love, slice the bread." She was about to sit down when she suddenly stopped and dashed back into the house. A moment later she emerged carrying a steaming white pot in her oven-gloved hands.

"Almost forgot," she said, setting it on the table. Wicky winked at Joyce.

"Told you!" he whispered, jerking his head at the pot. "Sticky toffee pud!" Joyce grinned back at him.

"Tuck in, Joyce," said Aggie. "Try an egg sandwich. We've got the best fairy chickens in Wheatby, though I say so myself."

Joyce hadn't realized quite how hungry flying all day had made her until she bit into a lovely, creamy egg salad sandwich. It was delicious. Aggie and Wicky had finished their supper long before Joyce finished hers.

"You must have been famished," laughed Aggie as Joyce scraped out her bowl from her second helping of pudding. Wicky cleared the plates from the table and took them inside the house. When he returned, he was carrying Joyce's map in his hand. He put it on the table, sat down in his chair, and began to fill a pipe with tobacco from a stone jar.

"Now then, young lady," he said, tamping the tobacco down in the bowl of his pipe with his thumb. "Let's hear all about you and find out how we can help."

Joyce told them everything that had happened since she'd left Swinley Hope and the Wickhams listened, their eyes stretching wider with every turn.

"So, you can see, I have to get to London," she said as she finished her tale.

"Yes, you do," agreed Wicky, putting his spectacles on and unfolding the map. "Let's see. Right, here's Wheatby and there's Millets Mountain. I can't really think of any landmarks between here and there, but you can see its peak quite clearly in daylight."

"Thank you," said Joyce, stifling a yawn. "But I can't wait till morning. Isn't there any way of finding it tonight? I really have to keep going."

Aggie smiled at her. "We know you're in a hurry, dear, but how will you know if you're going the right way if you can't see the mountain? You won't be able to help the unicorn if you have an accident or get lost, will you? Stay with us tonight. We have a lovely guest room and you'll fly better if you're well rested. Wicky'll see you off at dawn."

Joyce knew that Aggie was right. Her wings felt weak and shaky and she could do with a good night's sleep. "Thank you," she said. "I'd love to stay."

Aggie went inside and emerged a moment later with pillows and a quilt. She led Joyce through the garden to a little clearing.

"Here we are," laughed Aggie. "Have you ever slept in a hammock before?"

Joyce shook her head. "Never!"

"Well, you're in for a treat."

Joyce looked doubtfully at the hammock. One end of it was tied to a hook on the cottage wall; the other was fastened to a post. Aggie lay the pillows and quilt in the hammock and helped Joyce climb in, making sure she had her wings wrapped comfortably around her, then she put the quilt over the top and tucked it in at the sides.

"Sleep well, my dear," she said. "And don't worry, Wicky will make sure you're on your way nice and early in the morning. Night-night."

"G'night, and thanks." Joyce yawned. Even though she was exhausted she didn't go to sleep immediately. For a little while she lay in the hammock and stared at the stars, seeking out the constellations. She could see so many of them. There was Cepheus the King and, close by, Cassiopeia the Queen, and there in the middle of the sky was Hercules. It was a perfect night for stargazing, but she couldn't keep her eyes open for long, and soon the soft swaying of the hammock and the warm evening air lulled her into a wonderfully deep and restful sleep.

By three a.m. the next morning almost everyone in Buckingham Palace was tucked up in their beds fast asleep. Merrie wasn't. Merrie was wide awake and sitting on her bed in her small but lavishly decorated bedroom. She had changed out of her neat black dress and was now wearing a vermilion negligee with turquoise lace trim and a purple turban stretched over the orange curlers all over her head. She was smoking a thin brown cigarette and squinting through the smoke at a glossy catalog full of pictures of fabulous houses for sale. When she found one she liked, she ripped out the page. There were several pages strewn about the bed.

Her laptop was open and balanced on her lap. Merrie glanced at the clock on her bedside table. It was a quarter after three.

"Nine fifteen a.m. in the U.S. of A.," she said as she flung the catalog on the bed and snatched up her cell phone. Taking one last long drag of her cigarette, she dropped it in a dirty cup. It hissed as it hit the cocoa dregs in the bottom. Merrie cleared her throat, put a smile on her face, and dialed the number for the J. J. Rosenthal Institute in Columbus, Indiana.

Chapter 14

OVER THE HILLS AND FAR AWAY

"Joyce?"

Joyce opened her eyes to find Aggie Wickham smiling at her. "I've brought you a cup of tea," she said as she set a little china mug on a stool beside the hammock. "Breakfast's ready when you are," she called as she headed to the house.

Joyce stretched luxuriously. She'd slept well. Now it was time to get going. It was then that she discovered that the easiest way to get out of a hammock is to fall out. She stood up quickly and dusted off her crumpled clothes. She'd been so tired the night before that she hadn't even bothered to take off her dress, and she looked such a state that she wondered what the posh Wheatby fairies would make of her now.

The Wickhams' kitchen was a cheerful little room with cream-colored walls and pale blue cupboards. Yellow gingham curtains hung at the window and seemed to fill the room with sunlight even before dawn. Everything about the room was neat and tidy— everything except a rolltop desk in the corner. It was littered with books, files, papers, and piles of odds and ends. Every drawer was open a bit as though too full to close all the way. It was strange to see such a thing in an otherwise immaculate room.

Wicky was at the table when Joyce entered. He smiled up at her and nodded his good morning, but he didn't speak because he had his mouth full. He was in his police uniform again and was studying her map while he ate.

"Sit down, love," said Aggie, lifting a fried egg out of a pan with a spatula and sliding it onto a plate. "Eat up. You'll need all your strength. It's a good day's journey to Millets Mountain."

Wicky wiped his mouth on a napkin and pushed his plate to one side.

"Now, Joyce," he said in a serious tone. "I can see the logic of your taking the most direct route to

London, and the first part—Wheatby to Millets Mountain, to . . . ah, yes . . . to Shillings, right there." He tapped at a town on the map. "That's all well and good, but after Shillings—hmmm, I know from this it looks like you'd reach London faster if you just carried on flying east, in a straight line, but that's not actually the best way."

"Why not?" asked Joyce, looking at the map.

"Because," Wicky went on, "you'll be flying over some areas that are a little . . . what shall we say . . . er . . . dangerous, even in the daytime. I strongly advise you not to go that way."

"But it'll take too long to go around," replied Joyce.

"Not as long as it'll take if you get robbed or kidnapped," warned Wicky.

"Don't frighten the child," said Aggie.

"I don't mean to," replied Wicky. "But I want her to be safe."

"How do I avoid these areas then?" asked Joyce.

"Your best bet would be to go south after Shilling." He pointed to one of the blue lines. "That way," he continued, "you'll miss flying over Motton Moor— you definitely want to avoid that. It's a nasty place, full of fog and tricky types. And you'll avoid the rougher areas of Clangton and Shodworth, too. After Begby Mill you go north to Hannam Rise. You'll be able to see London from the top of there. Here, I'll write it all down for you on the back of the map." Wicky turned the map over and, using an old-fashioned ink pen, began to jot down his directions. When he'd finished, he blew on the ink to dry it and folded up the map. Joyce thanked him and put it back in her canvas bag.

"Wait, there's another thing. You won't know which way you're going without a compass," said Wicky, getting up and going to the messy rolltop desk in the corner. He started to rummage in the drawers. "I know I had one here somewhere."

"Well, if you ever organized that desk . . . ," teased Aggie, winking at Joyce.

"It is organized," responded the policeman. "You just don't understand my system. Aha! See, I told you!" He handed Joyce a small pocket compass and sat beside her to show her how to use it.

"Here's some sandwiches," said Aggie, handing Joyce a little package. "They're egg salad because you seemed to like those so much last night." Joyce thanked her and put the package in her bag. Wicky held the door open for her and Aggie followed them outside. "And here's a flask of hot tea in case you need a pick-me-up. You can keep the flask or return it someday, as you like."

"You're very kind, thank you," said Joyce, putting the flask in her bag. She felt overwhelmed with gratitude. "I wish there was something I could do to repay you."

"You're already doing a lot for us," said Wicky.

"I am? How?" asked Joyce.

Aggie smiled. "By doing what you know has to be done. By risking your neck to fetch back the unicorn and save your forest."

"But I still don't understand—"

"Because," said Aggie, explaining, "I believe that when someone does something good in the world, it has repercussions. It affects all of us, makes us all feel better to know that someone like you is out there."

"But I have to do this. I told you, it was my fault that the unicorn was discovered."

"Yes, but you chose to undertake this journey, didn't you?"

"And," added Wicky, "your taking this on makes us feel happier about the world. Now, come along, we'd better hurry before there are too many early-bird busybody fairies flying around. I'll be out of a job if they find out I didn't clap you in irons."

"They couldn't fire you!" gasped Joyce, horrified.

"I'd like to see them try," laughed Wicky.

"Goodbye then, Joyce dear," said Aggie, hugging her tight. "Good luck. And any time you're passing you must come and visit us again."

Wicky put on his policeman's helmet, took hold of Joyce's hand, and flapped his big gray wings. In a moment, they were airborne.

Above them the sky was still indigo, but to the east the dawn was breaking. The air was absolutely still. Joyce gazed at the town below her. Barely a light showed in any of the houses. The yellow street lamps burned as they had all night. At the clock tower Wicky veered to the left and flew above the main street that yesterday had been crowded with people below and fairies above. Now it was empty.

Wicky headed to the roof of the tallest building and landed close to where Joyce had stood the previous evening. The sky was fully light now, making the whole town and all the surrounding countryside visible.

"Not a bad view," said Wicky, his eyes scouring the horizon. "Ah, there it is," he exclaimed, pointing east. "That's Millets Mountain."

Beyond the town an immense plain of rolling fields interspersed with dark hedgerows stretched into the distance. Joyce couldn't see anything that looked like a mountain. The horizon was absolutely flat save for a minute blip sticking up. Joyce stared harder. Was that the mountain?

Wicky laughed when he saw her face. "Doesn't look like much from here," he said. "But it'll be enough to guide you and it'll grow bigger the closer you get. It's a fair way to fly on a hot day, so take it slow and steady. After you get to the mountain, just follow the route I drew on your map and you'll be in London soon enough."

Joyce gave the policeman a big hug. "Thank you," she said. "Thank you for all your help."

"Oh, you are very welcome, my dear," Wicky said with a smile. "Fly safe."

Joyce spread her wings and launched herself off the flat roof. With a final wave to Wicky, she turned and headed toward the blip on the horizon.

Chapter 15

WARNING WOOD

Joyce flew all day without stopping. After Wheatby, the landscape was made up of irregularly shaped fields. Every now and then she saw a small lake, a cluster of farm buildings, or the odd village, but mostly it was just one field after another. Once the monotony was broken by the interesting sight of a large racetrack where trainers were running horses around the track. Later she flew over a wonderful, stately home with formal gardens and fountains.

For the longest time Joyce felt that she wasn't getting any closer to her destination. All day long the mountain seemed to remain a distant blip on the horizon, never getting any more mountain-like in size. But by the late afternoon, after hours of hard flying and watching the land slip by below, Joyce looked up and was shocked to see that Millets Mountain was suddenly much bigger. Joyce was glad because she was starving. Aggie's sandwiches were still in her bag. She was looking forward to having them when she reached the mountain.

It was early evening by the time she made it to the barren top of Millets Mountain. She flew around to the eastern side of the mountain, where she landed on a large rock, pulled the sandwiches out of her bag, and stared eastward while she ate.

Over the course of her first full day at the palace, Princess Eleanor got to visit the unicorn no less than five times. She saw him for an hour before breakfast, then Merrie told her to pop down during her morning recess and check that he was all right.

At lunchtime Merrie thoughtfully suggested they take a picnic to the indoor riding school and let Lemon and the unicorn have a little run about— providing, of course, that Hobbs and Captain Simperington were there to make sure that no one came into the indoor school and saw the unicorn. Merrie had been in a very playful mood and had even brought a large blow-up exercise ball into the ring. The princess, the unicorn, and Lemon had a great time chasing it around, at least until the unicorn accidentally popped it with his horn. The princess was a little afraid that Merrie would be annoyed, but to her amazement the governess just laughed and said it didn't matter. After that the unicorn had run around the ring with the popped ball on his horn, stopping every now and then as if to taunt the princess and try to get her to pull it off him. That had been a very fun hour.

After lunch Merrie had let Eleanor skip the afternoon's second lesson (American poetry studies) and go and help Hobbs muck out the stall again. Then for the fifth and final visit of the day Merrie took Eleanor to say good night to the unicorn and Lemon and check that everything was as it should be.

It had been an absolutely perfect day, except . . . except that on that last visit of the day Eleanor had felt a vague, niggling worry. It was hard to describe. She watched the unicorn closely as he pulled hay from the hayrack. There didn't seem to be anything wrong with him. He still looked the same. He still behaved in the same playful manner. He still had that cheeky glint in his brown eyes. Even so, she couldn't shake the feeling that something was not quite right.

She tried to explain her feelings to Merrie as they

made their way up the palace stairs to the princess's bedchamber.

"Don't worry," advised Merrie, then after a quick glance about, she lowered her voice and whispered, "Your unicorn has just had a wonderful and thoroughly enjoyable day, Princess Baby. He is the picture of health and he certainly doesn't look unhappy. Honestly, my love, what could possibly be wrong?"

"I don't know," replied the princess.

"I think you may just be tired, my love," suggested Merrie cheerily. "You've had an exhausting day and the sooner you're asleep the better, I think."

Princess Eleanor nodded and yawned. Merrie was right. She was tired. She couldn't wait to get into bed.

Just as Merrie opened Eleanor's door, the governess's purple phone beeped. Merrie pulled it out and quickly glanced at the screen.

"Have you got a message?" asked Eleanor.

"Dear me, no," replied Merrie, slipping the phone back in her pocket. "Who'd be sending me messages, for goodness' sake? It's just telling me the battery's low." Merrie gently pushed the princess through the bedroom door.

"In the bath with you, my love," she said, propelling Eleanor toward the bathroom. Merrie left her there and beetled across the room and through the study door. "I just have to pop over and get my laptop from my desk. Should only take ten minutes or so to go over tomorrow's schedule, then you can go straight to sleep. Back in a mo!"

Do we really have to do the schedule now? thought Eleanor, yawning. She turned to protest and caught sight of her governess through the open study door. Merrie had her phone open in her hand. Her eyes were glinting as she read whatever was written there.

Merrie must have had a message after all, thought the princess as she went into the bathroom. Who on earth, she wondered, could it be from?

From the top of Millets Mountain everything on the ground looked smaller than fairy-sized. At the foot of the mountain was a busy gray road with several lanes of traffic. Tiny cars and trucks raced along it. Joyce noticed that as the road headed south, it cut right through the middle of a large forest. She looked at her map. The road wasn't marked on it, though the forest was. It was called Warning Wood. Joyce wondered why the humans had split a lovely old forest in two. She noticed the trees on the north side of the road looked different than the ones on the south. They were darker.

In the far distance she could just make out the huge gray sprawl of a large town. That must be Shilling, she thought as she studied the map.

Looking at the map reminded her of how far she had to go until she got to London. I'm not going to think about that, she told herself, folding up the map and putting it back in her bag. I'm tired, and everything always seems far more difficult when you're tired.

Once she'd eaten Aggie's sandwiches, she felt much better. She thought she was done with flying for the day and planned to spend the night on top of the mountain, but just after the sun set a warm wind started to blow from the west and ominous dark clouds appeared on the horizon. Joyce could hear thunder in the distance. She stared at the dark clouds and saw a fork of lightning shoot through them. The storm was headed her way and there was nowhere to shelter on the bare mountaintop.

Where could she go? She looked at the land beneath her. That forest, the one with the road going through it, wasn't so far away. It would take her off course a little way, but she'd still be able to see Shilling in the morning and she had the map, the compass, and Wicky's directions.

With no time to lose, she flew off the mountain

and, with the warm wind at her back, headed for Warning Wood.

The first trees she came to were black and leafless, and the sight made her uneasy. Bare trees in the middle of summer? she thought. That's not right. She flew on, determined to find a better place to shelter from the storm.

But there wasn't time. The heavens were suddenly and violently ripped apart as the storm struck. Joyce screamed in midair as one massive jagged bolt shot past just a few feet in front of her. Then the thunder clapped with earsplitting volume, and it began to rain. Within moments Joyce was soaked through. Soon her wings would fail her. Bare trees or not, she had no choice.

Perhaps it won't be that bad in here, she thought as she flew past the dark branches. Unfortunately, it was a lot worse. In the next flash of lightning she saw that the trees weren't just bare. They were diseased. They were dying. Trunks were gnarled and twisted. Branches were torn and mangled. Blackened leaves were caught against twisted twigs like burnt litter in a chain-link fence. Everywhere rotten bark hung in tattered shreds.

Joyce landed in the middle of a muddy clearing and ran to the shelter of the nearest tree. When she reached it, she found a little fairy house built into the bark, just like the ones back home in Swinley Hope, except that it wasn't quite the same. This house had been abandoned. It was a ruin. The shutters were smashed, and the door had fallen off its hinges and lay on the ground. Joyce went inside, hoping to find shelter for the night, but the house was uninhabitable. All the walls and the furniture were covered with mold and the smell was overpowering. Joyce turned to go.

The rain was coming down hard. She sheltered in the doorway looking out, and with each flash of lightning, she saw evidence of other fairy houses in the other trees—all of them in ruins, all of them abandoned. This was a town once, she thought. She sat down on the doorstep and, wrapping her wet wings around her, stared out at the rain until the sound of it lulled her to sleep.

In his sleek, modern office at the headquarters of the J. J. Rosenthal Institute in Columbus, Indiana, Professor Cregg Wursteinmunster picked up his golf bag and was about to leave for the day when the telephone rang. Professor Wursteinmunster groaned, but he could not resist returning to look at the caller I.D. number on the telephone.

"International," he mused. "Could be important."

He put down his golf clubs and picked up the receiver.

"Hello, Professor Wursteinmunster speaking," he said importantly.

A high-toned English accent blasted through the receiver. "Professor Wursteinmunster? Margaret Merrieweather here. I left a message on your voice mail yesterday after I'd e-mailed you some interesting photographs. I'm wondering why you have not yet returned my call."

The professor screwed up his eyes and squeezed the bridge of his nose with his thumb and forefinger as though in pain. Why had he picked up the phone? He recognized the woman's shrill, pretentious voice. Her message on his voice mail had been long and very complicated. "Ah, yes, Mrs. Merrieweather—"

"It's 'miss,' " Merrie corrected him.

"Excuse me?"

"*Miss* Merrieweather." Merrie giggled girlishly.

"Ah, is it? Well, Miss Merrieweather . . . ," Professor Wursteinmunster sighed. He knew what was coming. He received dozens of such calls a day. "Are you, by chance, calling about a supernatural animal of some sort?"

"Yes! A unicorn!" Merrie squealed.

The professor rolled his eyes. "A unicorn? How

extraordinary," he replied in a voice that suggested there was nothing extraordinary about Merrie's revelation.

"Yes! It's a male, a stallion. A splendid, spectacular beast." Merrie's voice hardened imperceptibly. "Didn't you look at my e-mail?" she inquired.

"No, I'm afraid I haven't gotten to it yet," sighed the professor, gazing out the window at the golf course in the distance. "Now where did you say you saw this animal?"

"I didn't just see it," replied Merrie. "I caught it. Well, not me personally, I had someone do it for me, but I caught it and I—"

"Mmm . . . hmm," said the professor, picking a piece of lint off his brightly colored golfing sweater. "Caught it, did you?"

"Not only did I catch it, but the animal is"— Merrie's voice dropped to a whisper—"at this very moment installed in the Royal stables at Buckingham Palace."

"In London?" snorted the professor.

"Yes, in London, how many Buckingham Palaces do you think there are?" Merrie snapped. The professor jerked the phone away from his ear. He didn't need this. He was about to hang up when the Merrieweather woman spoke again. "Now, professor," she said sweetly. "Regarding the million-dollar reward for any proof of—"

"Ah—excuse me. I must stop you there, Miss Merrieweather." The professor smiled. They'd reached the only part of these calls the professor always enjoyed—telling these gold-digging geeks that the institute wasn't just going to hand them a million dollars for a few cobbled-together photos of the Loch Ness Monster. "Regarding the reward, I'm sure you understand that there are a good many steps to go through before we hand over any money. We require irrefutable proof, which means that the animal in question must be thoroughly examined by our team of highly trained scientific investigators and crypto-zoologists. We receive a great many calls about this reward and you might want to look at our Web site if you require further assistance. Thank you. Good night."

"Not so fast," snapped Merrie. "You're not dealing with some wet-behind-the-ears college nerd now. I happen to be not only a highly respected member of the Royal household, but also a close confidant of Their Majesties. They have entrusted to me the care and education of their only daughter, Her Royal Highness, Princess Eleanor."

"You mean you're the nanny?" scoffed the professor.

"Governess!" snapped Merrie. "My position

within the palace is hardly the point. I think you might want to check your e-mail, Professor Clever Clogs, and I recommend that you do so immediately. Be assured that if I don't hear from you within the next ten minutes, I will be offering this information to Ansgar Arnesson. I'm sure the noted Swedish scientist will be more than interested in this matter. The telephone number of my private line is in the message with the photographs. Goodbye." And with that she hung up.

"Arrghhhhhhh!" yelled Professor Wursteinmunster as he slammed the phone down and flumped back into his chair. Golf would have to wait. The woman might not have anything, but if she did, and if she gave it to Arnesson . . . The professor shuddered. The woman had touched a nerve. Ansgar Arnesson was J. J. Rosenthal's oldest and most despised enemy. Cregg Wursteinmunster clicked angrily on his junk-mail folder and scrolled to Merrie's e-mail. He was pretty certain the woman was a fruit loop, but just in case . . . He hit return, the e-mail opened, and Merrie's photographs of the Swinley Forest unicorn instantly appeared.

"Holy moly," exclaimed the professor under his breath. Without taking his eyes from the screen, he reached for the telephone, jabbed in three numbers, and put the receiver to his ear. "Hakim?" he yelled excitedly. "Get up here. No, forget golf. Ya gotta see this."

In her bedroom, Merrie wrapped her violet bed jacket around her and sat back against her cushions. She calmly lit a cigarette and picked up two of the pages she'd torn from the Realtor's catalog.

"Ooh, that million dollars is so mine," she said to herself as she perused the pictures. "Hmmm. Shall I have a villa in Portugal or Spain? Portugala or Española?" Before she could decide, her cell phone rang. Cregg Wursteinmunster was back on the line. Margaret Merrieweather smiled, puffed on her cigarette, and let the phone ring and ring and ring.

Chapter 16

Motton Moor

Joyce woke at dawn to the sound of crows cawing in the bare trees above her. The rain had stopped and the sun was shining, but the dying trees didn't look any better than they had the night before, and the smell of mold and rotten vegetation seemed even worse. Joyce didn't want to hang about. She unwrapped herself from her wings and shook out the crumples. Her wings were still a little damp, but they would soon dry in the sun.

She reached for her canvas bag. It was soaking wet and so was everything in it. Worst of all, her map was ruined. All the beautiful little watercolor paintings had dissolved and run together and were now just one muddy smudge. The landmarks, the rivers, the towns, the palace, and all the neatly written place names— gone. Joyce tried to be positive. At least she still had the compass and Wicky's directions. But when she looked on the back of the map she found that the rain had turned Wicky's list into a big blue blur. Joyce stared at it in disbelief. Now she didn't know where to go.

She tried to think. There had to be a way. She looked at the compass in her hand. London was east of Shilling, she remembered that much. The compass could guide her in that direction. Wicky hadn't wanted her to go directly to London. He'd said that it would be dangerous, but she didn't have any other choice now. She would have to risk it.

Joyce closed her fingers around the compass and took off flying through the bare branches toward the bright sky.

Once she was above the ruined forest, she noticed again what she'd seen from the top of Millets Mountain. Only half of Warning Wood was dying. The great gray road cut the forest in two and the trees on the far side appeared to be thriving.

Joyce puzzled over this, and then, suddenly, she understood. A forest can't survive without its unicorn.

There was no way across that road. The unicorn of Warning Wood must be stuck on the far side of it. He couldn't get to the part that was dying. He couldn't save it.

The dying trees, the town the fairies had abandoned—this was what would happen to Swinley Forest if she didn't find their unicorn and bring him home. Joyce knew she couldn't let that happen. She kicked her feet, furiously flapped her wings, and flew toward Shilling.

The next morning the princess awoke bright and refreshed and not at all tired, but when she went with Merrie and Simpers to see the unicorn after breakfast, she still felt uneasy. She'd brought more sugar carrots and Lemon was already chomping greedily through hers, but the unicorn didn't seem to want one. He would take it from her outstretched hand but kept dropping it. Every time he did, the princess picked it up and tried again.

"You know you like them," she said encouragingly. "Yum! Yum!" But the unicorn still wouldn't eat his carrot.

The princess was puzzled. He'd happily eaten all the sugar carrots she'd given him the day before.

"Not hungry, eh?" she said as she smoothed his beautiful mane with her hand. "Shall I take you for a walk later? We could go around the palace gardens, just you and I. Wouldn't that be nice?" The unicorn snorted softly and nibbled affectionately at her collar.

"Merrie?" asked the princess as she picked up the unwanted carrot for the umpteenth time. "Does the unicorn look different to you today?"

"No, my darling," replied Merrie, smiling at the princess. "He looks as splendid as ever, and he's obviously so happy to be with you."

"I'll be back this afternoon, I promise," whispered the princess, reaching up and gently scratching the unicorn behind the ear. She kissed him once more, then left him in the stall and walked away.

"Merrie?" asked the princess when she had gone a few yards down the stable. When Merrie didn't respond, Princess Eleanor turned and was surprised to see her still standing at the stall door. The governess's white face looked pinched and tight, and her eyes, beneath the frowning brows, were dark with concentration. Her lips twitched and her fingers picked at something on her chin.

"Merrie?" asked Eleanor.

"I . . . er . . . ," stammered Merrie. "So sorry, my

dear, I was miles away. Let's to lessons, forthwith!"
She jerked the sackcloth curtain shut, then scuttled to
the princess's side and hurried her out of the stables.

When Joyce reached the town of Shilling, she didn't
stop to take a rest. She checked the compass to make
sure of her course and flew on. She didn't take a break
until mid-afternoon, by which time she was exhausted.

She landed on a shady island at the edge of a blue
lake and paddled her toes in the water. Her island was
really just a moss-covered rock hidden in the reeds,
but for her it was perfect. She lay back on the soft
moss and stared up at the clear sky. Just fifteen minutes, she promised herself as she drifted off to sleep.

When Joyce awoke, she was shocked to find the
sky full of fiery orange and pink clouds. It was already
evening. She stood up quickly, cross with herself for
wasting so much time. She washed her hands and face
in the lake, then, with a quick check of the compass,
took to the air.

The sky was fully dark when Joyce noticed that
the land she was flying over was covered in a dense,
swirling fog. A shudder of revulsion passed through
her, and she suddenly remembered how Wicky had
mentioned a nasty place full of "fog and tricky types,"
a place to be avoided. What had he called it? Motton

Moor. Instinctively, Joyce knew this was where she was. Wicky had been right. It would have been better to avoid the moor, but she had no choice now. Turning back and trying to go around it would take too long. It was best to keep going and hope that Motton Moor wasn't too big.

The air grew colder, and before long Joyce's teeth were chattering and her fingertips had turned blue. Thinking it might warm her to fly a bit faster, she flapped her wings more forcefully. Unfortunately, she had been flying for so long and had been working her wings so hard that when she increased her flapping rate something terrible happened.

The muscles in her left wing cramped! Joyce folded her painful wing in and held it to her body to protect it. Now she was flying on only one wing, which really meant that she was falling—fast. She was spinning toward the mists in a tight spiral.

It was almost midnight and Princess Eleanor was still wide awake in her opulent queen-sized bed in her palace bedroom. She was staring up at the little gold cherubs on the canopy, but she wasn't really seeing them.

She was thinking about the unicorn and the un-easy feeling that was stronger than ever. She hadn't seen him all day—not since that morning, in fact. She felt bad that she'd broken her promise to take him for a walk. She had meant to, but when she asked Merrie if she could go, Merrie had said she was very sorry but she'd forgotten there was to be a Royal garden party in the palace garden this afternoon, so it would be impossible to take the unicorn out. "Perhaps later!" Merrie had said. Eleanor heard nothing but "perhaps later" all day. Later never came.

After her schoolwork was done, she had a dress fitting, then a portrait sitting, and then she had to have her tea. After tea, one of the cooks insisted on teaching her how to make almond cookies, and then an hour before bedtime, just when everything had calmed down and Eleanor was about to go to the stables to say good night, Merrie had suddenly burst in chattering excitedly and hurrying the princess into a pretty evening frock. Plans had been changed, arrangements had been made, and the princess, as an extra special treat, was to go to the theater to see *Romeo and Juliet* and after the play she was to be introduced to the whole cast. This was a wonderful surprise. Next to horses (and now unicorns), attending the theater was her favorite thing in the world. Eleanor loved Shakespeare's plays with a passion, and though she'd read *Romeo and Juliet* many times, she'd never actually seen it performed onstage. She was very excited. How could she not go? She promised herself she would go see the unicorn as soon as she got home.

But when she got home, Merrie wouldn't hear of her going to the stables at such an hour, and she'd been hustled off to bed.

The princess was staring at the cherubs' fat-cheeked faces when the idea of sneaking down to the stables suddenly occurred to her. She glanced at her clock. It was very late, just past midnight, but she was wide awake. Why not? Most of the Royal household would be asleep. She could easily sneak down and check on him, couldn't she? No one would ever know.

Eleanor got out of bed, put on her robe, then felt for her slippers with her feet. They weren't in their usual place beside the bed. She bent down to look but they were nowhere to be seen. Then she looked in her closet and discovered that all of her shoes had disappeared. All of them.

Perhaps Merrie had sent them to be cleaned, she thought. But why send all of them at once? They couldn't all have been dirty. And what about her slippers? They were brand-new. It was very odd.

Eleanor thought for a moment. She didn't want to go to the stables without shoes because the cobbles would be rough underfoot. She just needed something to wear on her feet—anything would do. Suddenly she remembered the mudroom below stairs. No doubt she'd find a pair of boots in there.

She cinched her robe around her waist and padded barefoot across her bedroom. Very quietly, she opened the door an inch or two and peered out to see if the coast was clear. It wasn't—Merrie was coming down the corridor. Eleanor shrank back, pulled the door almost shut, and watched through the gap.

This was a very different Merrie from the one she saw every day. This Merrie had curlers in her hair, cream all over her face, and was wearing a vermilion lace negligee with slippers to match. This Merrie was carrying a mug in one hand and a platter of cookies in the other. This Merrie was dancing a cha-cha-cha and singing, "I'm in the moohooood for love," very out of tune.

Once Merrie had danced out of sight around the corner, the princess turned the other way and hurried toward the main stairs. If she met anyone, she told herself, she would remember that she was a Royal princess and tell them to mind their own beeswax. She'd read that in a book and she thought it was very funny and not too rude.

She saw no one until, when she was halfway down the stairs, a footman on night duty came out of one of the reception rooms carrying a tray of used china. Eleanor instantly ducked behind the balustrade and then got cross with herself. For heaven's sakes, this is my parents' palace, she thought. I am a princess. Even so, she stayed low until the footman had crossed the black and white checkered marble floor and vanished through another door on the left.

At the bottom of the stairs, she ran across the hall and listened at the door the footman had used. After a moment, she opened it, slipped inside, and closed it quietly behind her.

The corridors below stairs reeked of cabbage and disinfectant. Eleanor snuck into the kitchen and grabbed a handful of brown sugar from the big stone sugar jar, then she hurried to the mudroom, where she quickly found her Wellies and put them on. The large rain boots looked pretty ridiculous with her dressing gown, but this wasn't the time to worry about such things. She was just opening the door to the kitchen yard when she ran smack into Neville Garstang, the second under-butler, who, thinking she was one of the servants' children, grabbed her roughly by the arm.

" 'Ere, what's your game?" he snarled. His breath

smelled of whiskey and tobacco. Eleanor was frightened and tried to pull away, but Garstang held on tight. "Kid like you needs a good spanking."

"I—I—I—" stammered the princess. Garstang was a tall, lanky fellow with vicious eyes. He looked more than capable of doling out a good spanking. Eleanor realized that she couldn't pull away from him; the man was too strong. She would have to try another tactic. *I am a princess,* she told herself. *I am a Royal princess.* Suddenly she was not in the least bit afraid.

"Let's see your 'orrible face, then," Garstang said as he flicked on the light. Suddenly all the color drained out of his face.

"Oh, I . . . er . . . I do beg your pardon, Your 'Ighness," he said, recovering as much as he could. "I did not recognize you, miss."

Princess Eleanor pulled herself up to her full height and stared, unblinking, into the man's eyes. "Obviously," she said imperiously.

"Is there anything I can get for you, miss?" groveled Garstang. "Some warm milk? Cake? Chocolate?"

"No thank you, Garstang," replied Eleanor with icy politeness. She knew she probably looked ridiculous in her dressing gown and Wellies, but she wasn't going to let that bother her. "Please let me pass," she commanded calmly. On the outside she maintained an icy manner, but inside she wanted to giggle. She had never actually tried behaving this way before. She was amazed at just how effective it was.

Garstang bowed and moved out of her way.

"Thank you," she said. "And, Garstang?" she added, pausing at the door and looking back.

"Yes, miss?"

"Don't tell anyone you've seen me. I think you'll agree where I've been and what I'm doing is none of your beeswax, is it?"

"Very good, miss."

Then, with her head held high, Eleanor passed through the door and walked out into the warm night air.

Back in the mudroom Neville Garstang narrowed his eyes as he watched her cross the yard and enter the stable building. Slowly he nodded his head. The second under-butler was one of many on the palace staff who earned a pretty penny by keeping Margaret Merrieweather informed of the goings-on about the place.

"Right, Your Royal 'Ighness!" he said as he fastened his top button, straightened his hair, and made for the back stairs. "I wonder if your governess knows what you're up to. Should be worth a tenner or more. None of my beeswax indeed!"

Princess Eleanor had never been in the stables on

her own after dark, and she had to admit that even in her new courageous princess frame of mind it was still a bit too spooky. The only light came from the electric Insect-O-Cutors™ spaced along the walls. The rest of the stable building was in shadow. Every so often the eerie blue lights flickered as they zapped a moth or mosquito that had flown too close. Eleanor jumped each time this happened.

"It's just the stables," she told herself sternly. "Nothing to be scared of here."

She breathed in the lovely smell of horse and hay and heard a few comforting footfalls and soft snorts from the stalls on either side. Battery-operated lanterns hung on hooks just outside the tack room to be used in the unlikely event of a power outage. Eleanor took one down, switched it on, and then set it down beside her. A box of carrots stood on the bench. She reached in and took two, then she rolled them in the brown sugar, which was now warm and sticky in her hand.

Lantern in one hand, sugar carrots in the other, she slowly made her way along the wide, cobbled aisle between the stalls. On either side of her, horses came to their doors to see if she had food for them. Some of the more expensive Thoroughbreds shook their heads, flaring their nostrils and rolling their eyes to let her know they didn't like having their sleep disturbed.

"Sorry, sorry," said Eleanor. "Shush."

When she reached the last stall, Lemon was waiting for her with her head poking through the sackcloth curtains and hanging over the half door. Good old Lemon; she must have recognized her footsteps. It was odd, but there seemed to be a light on in the stall. Perhaps Hobbs left it on for some reason, she thought.

"Hello, Lemony," she said as she scratched under her chin. Lemon pushed at her with her nose, eagerly searching for carrots or sugar cubes. "Whoa, give me a minute," she said, bringing out one of the carrots. The pony's fumbling lips snaffled it up.

The princess slid the bolt and opened the half door. Lemon obediently backed away. The princess ducked under the curtain. "Now where's that uni— Oh!"

She stopped dead. The unicorn stood in the corner of the stall. Hobbs and Captain Simperington were with him. The captain was holding up a feed bucket, trying to get the unicorn to eat. Hobbs was applying something to the unicorn's hooves. He stood up when he saw the princess. Both men bowed.

"Good evening, Your Highness," said the captain politely.

The princess didn't answer. She couldn't. The shock of the unicorn's appearance had taken all her words away. What had happened to him? He looked so ill. His coat was dull, and there were dark mottled spots on his golden horn and hooves. His eyes were no longer bright, but when he saw her, a faint gleam returned to them, and he snorted softly.

Eleanor's heart ached and the lump in her throat felt impossibly large. "What . . . what's wrong with him?" she asked in a trembling voice.

"We're not certain, miss," the captain answered quietly. "He's not eating, and his coat, as you can see, is molting. Hobbs has made up some ointment to put on his horn and his hooves. It might help."

"The captain thinks it might be an allergic reaction, miss," Hobbs suggested respectfully.

"To what, Simps?" she asked as she gently touched the unicorn's neck.

"I'm afraid we don't know, Your Highness," the captain replied sadly.

The princess stared at the unicorn. It hadn't been all that long since she'd seen him—she'd visited him just that morning, in fact—but he had changed so much. She'd thought then that his coat had looked slightly duller, that he'd seemed a little sad. She shouldn't have allowed herself to be persuaded that everything was fine. She should have heeded the uneasiness she'd felt. She should have come to see him when she'd promised.

The princess suddenly burst into tears and buried her face in the unicorn's dull, dry mane.

"Oh, Your HIGHNESS!" cried Merrie as she rushed into the stall. Her sudden appearance spooked Lemon, and the little pony shied, whinnied loudly, then bolted to the farthest corner.

Eleanor almost bolted too when she saw Merrie rushing toward her with a big quilted blanket. Merrie had removed her rollers, and now her hair stood up in hard copper curls all over her head. She was wearing a sensible, plum-colored grandma-ish dressing gown, but it wasn't quite long enough to cover the negligee beneath, and a whisper of vermilion showed at the hem.

"Oh, Princess Baby, I've been so worried about you!" Merrie cried as she wrapped the blanket around Eleanor. "Back to bed, straightaway," Merrie bossed as she pulled the princess away from the unicorn and bundled her out of the stall. Eleanor was too upset to protest.

"You poor, poor thing," cooed Merrie as she hurried her along the cobbled aisle. "Please, don't cry, my darling."

"But, Merrie, he's so ill!" sobbed Eleanor.

"I know, my love, I know," said Merrie soothingly as they left the stable building and set off across the courtyard. "I'm so sorry. There, there!"

"I shouldn't have left him alone all day," cried the princess. "I should have come to see him."

"Don't worry, my Princess Baby," mollified Merrie. "Hobbs will make him better. You'll see. I'm certain your unicorn will be right as rain come morning."

Princess Eleanor shook her head. "No, Merrie," she said. "I think being here is what is making him ill—perhaps he's allergic to the stables or the city air."

"My love, that can't be it," said Merrie in a reasonable tone. "The Royal stables wouldn't make any animal sick. They are too well equipped for that. "

"But, Merrie," said the princess, "this isn't the unicorn's home. He belongs in the forest. Maybe if he goes back there, he'll get better."

Merrie shook her head and tutted. "What a lot of fuss, my Princess Baby," she chided. She spoke gently, but there was a slight tightness to her voice. "Come, come. Your unicorn's probably just caught a little cold. This is absolutely the best place for him. He *loves* being with you."

"I know," sighed the princess. "I love being with him, too, but I can't bear to see him suffer. I want Hobbs to take him back tonight, right now. And if Hobbs stays at Swinley, he can be near the forest every day to make sure the unicorn's all right. I'm going to go and ask him now."

"No, no you're not," snapped Merrie as she tightened her arm around the princess's shoulders. The princess blinked up at her, surprised. Merrie twisted her mouth into a more acceptable smile. "Sorry, my lamb, I didn't mean to snap, but it's very late and you need your rest. Let me take care of everything. I promise, as soon as I've seen you safely back to bed, I'll inform Hobbs of your wishes and make sure he carries them out immediately. Don't you worry about a thing. All righty?"

"But I'm not tired," protested Princess Eleanor as she yawned an enormous yawn. Merrie gave her shoulders a little squeeze.

"Let your Merrie take care of it, my dove. It's what I do." She smiled again, then, after a furtive glance back at the stables, she steered her exhausted Princess Baby toward the palace doors.

Beneath the mists of Motton Moor the ground was wet and marshy, but it still felt hard to Joyce when she crashed into it.

"Owwww!" she squealed. Her cramped wing was caught beneath her. She sat up and tried to stretch it out, but the pain was like two knives being pulled in opposite directions along the upper edge of the wing.

"Please," she thought, "please don't let it be

broken." Then she remembered that if she could move the wing, it wasn't broken—she tried to wiggle the very tip of it. It moved. That was a relief, but it still hurt—a lot. There was nothing for it. She would have to walk until her wing felt better. Very slowly Joyce got to her feet and sank up to her ankles in the squelchy ground.

The thick fog was everywhere, a white nothingness, and she couldn't see more than a foot in any direction. She took out the compass and tried to see the arrow in the dim light, but just as it settled Joyce thought she saw something, a shadow flitting through the white mist. She heard a noise behind her and spun around.

"Who's there?" she cried.

"Pigsies! Pigsies of Motton Moor!" sang a voice. "And we love, love, love to help the lonely traveler."

"Helpful little imps, we is," said another. There was giggling.

Imps? thought Joyce. Then her stomach turned to ice. They were shadow imps. She'd never seen any before, but she'd heard stories, and she knew that while all imps were bad, shadow imps were by far the worst.

She felt a tug on her hand, and suddenly the

compass was not there. The shadows giggled. "Give it back!" Joyce demanded.

"No!" said a small voice. "You don't need that here."

"We'll help you," sang another. Joyce pulled her hand away as cold fingers appeared through the mist and tried to latch on to hers.

"I don't want your help!" she cried. The fingers pulled away and vanished in the fog. "Please give me back my compass."

"Say pretty please—"

"Pretty please give me back my compass."

"Nope." The shadows laughed as though this was the funniest thing in the world. Joyce reached into the mist and tried to grab one of them, but the shadow imp was too quick for her.

"Don't worry, we'll sort you out," laughed a shadow.

"Sort you out good and proper."

"Get you off Motton Moor. Come along. Follow us."

"But I can hardly see you," said Joyce.

"That's the trouble with this fog . . ."

". . . it being night and all . . ."

". . . you can't see us . . ."

". . . you can't see anything."

"Then how am I supposed to follow you?" asked Joyce, exasperated.

"You'll have to use your ears, won't you?"

"Listen. Follow our voices, come on. This way, here we go. That's right," the voices called through the mist. And Joyce followed, trudging through the marshy ground in whatever direction they called from. Sometimes they seemed to be getting somewhere because the surface of the ground beneath her feet would change, becoming more or less marshy, and once or twice it became stony as though they'd succeeded in reaching dryer ground. Joyce had soon lost all sense of direction and began to suspect the imps weren't leading her anywhere at all.

When they took her across a shallow stream, only to lead her back over it half an hour later, Joyce's patience finally ran out.

"Enough!" she said, stopping abruptly. The shadows sniggered in the darkness. "You're just taking me around in circles." There was more sniggering.

Joyce folded her arms. "I'm not following you anymore."

There were groans of disappointment from the shadows. "But you have to!" said one. "How else are you going to get to where you're going?"

"I can fly," said Joyce, knowing full well that she

couldn't, not till her wing felt better. The shadows laughed.

"Go on, then."

Joyce didn't even try. The shadows laughed louder.

"Fly, my eye!" they snickered, thoroughly enjoying themselves now.

"You're not going anywhere, missy."

"You're staying here forever."

"The fog never goes away!"

"Even in daylight you won't find your way out of here."

"Not without our help, and you'll have to earn that now."

"No, I won't," said Joyce, sitting down on the wet ground, heartily sick and tired of playing this game. She could hear whispering in the mists, but she was past caring. She lay back and quite unexpectedly found herself staring up at the answer to her problems. The mists were not impenetrable in every direction.

Lying on the ground, looking up, Joyce could see right through the misty wisps to a sky that was crammed with stars. Now it was Joyce's turn to laugh. She knew the stars. She knew where they were supposed to be in the sky, and she could orient herself by them. Sam had taught her their names and she knew that the bright one there was called Polaris, or the North Star, and like the arrow on Wicky's compass, that star would show her the way. She was no longer lost.

"Time to go," she called out cheerily as she stood up and set off. Keeping the bright star on her left, she began to walk confidently across the marshy ground. The shadow imps were outraged.

"What's going on?" they whined.

"What's she doing?"

"She's leaving!"

"No! That's not fair!"

Joyce ignored them and kept on walking. It was almost one in the morning when she reached the edge of the moor. The ground began to slope upward. Soon Joyce was climbing out of the mist, grateful to be leaving the horrible moor behind her. She was very tired.

Half an hour later Merrie sat amongst the pillows on her bed, popped a whole custard cream cookie in her mouth, and glared at the purple cell phone on the bed beside her.

"Ring!" she commanded, spraying crumbs everywhere. "Ring! Ring! Ring!"

The cell phone remained silent. It neither rang, nor vibrated, nor beeped.

Merrie had been waiting for Professor Wursteinmunster to return her call for the past twenty-nine minutes.

Merrie lit another of her thin brown cigarettes, then jumped as the phone rang, its tinny ringtone loud in the silent room. Clearing her throat, she picked up the phone, flipped it open, and put it to her ear.

"Good evening, Professor," she said in her poshest voice. Her tone changed in an instant. "Arthur Glibson!" she groaned, rolling her eyes. "Get off the phone, for heaven's sakes. Yes, my new story's big. How big? Biggest I've given you in the past ten years, buggerlugs. Yes, Arthur, your readers will love it. No, no hints! You'll find out tomorrow. Be here at three—tradesmen's entrance! Of course you'll have the exclusive for your charming paper. Yes, I promised you, didn't I? Now get off! And don't phone again or I swear I'll clam up like a . . . a . . . well, like a clam. Goodbye!"

Merrie hung up and threw the phone across the bed. "Journalists!"

She lit a fresh cigarette off the end of the first, then jammed the stub in an open pot of face cream.

"Come on, Wursteinmunster!" she growled, glaring at the phone. It suddenly rang. Merrie scrambled across the bed to get it, accidentally dropping her cigarette amongst the papers on the bed as she answered the phone. She burned herself picking the cigarette up by the lit end.

"Oh, you idiot!" she said, quickly chucking the cold dregs of her hot chocolate over the papers to extinguish the sparks. "No, no, my dear Professor Wursteinmunster, of course I didn't call you an idiot. It must have been a crossed line. Yes, everything's fine. Just wanted to confirm you'll arrive by lunchtime tomorrow. Text me when you're landing and I'll meet you at the palace helipad. Goodbye—What? Oh? J. J. Rosenthal himself is coming with you and wants to offer me what?"

Merrie sat bolt upright, then jumped out of bed and began to pace the room. "Yes, Professor, I would seriously consider selling the unicorn. Yes, yes, once you verify his authentification. Whatever. And J.J.'s offer? Does that include the one-million-dollar reward? It doesn't? Well, that's very generous." Merrie's hand shook as she closed the phone.

"Twenty-one million dollars!" she whispered to herself as she sat down in a daze. She stared up at the ceiling. "Twenty-one mil from J.J., a couple of hundred thou cash from the press for all the exclusives, plus all my savings!" Her savings came from the money she'd earned from tattletaling on the Royals and was not an inconsiderable amount of cash. Merrie gasped incredulously. She was quiet for a minute as she totted it all up on her fingers, then her eyes stretched wide. "I am absolutely loaded," she gasped.

She laughed and grabbed the nearest real estate brochure and flicked through it. "Who wants a villa in Spain?" she scoffed. "I think a nice Italian palazzo would do. Oh, yes. That would be *molty benni*. *Si*, that would be *moltissimo bennissimo*!"

It felt good to be out of the dank mist on the moor, but Joyce was too tired to go much farther and her injured wing ached badly. She tried not to think about how she was going to get to London if she couldn't fly. I'll do it somehow, she thought. But for now she had to rest, if only for a little while. A rest would make her feel better—she hoped. By the dim starlight she looked around for somewhere comfortable to sleep.

A little farther up the slope there was a large bush with yellow flowers. Many of its petals had fallen and were scattered beneath it. They would make a fine bed. Joyce gathered them up into a big pile, then lay down on the makeshift mattress, buried herself in the petals, and fell fast asleep.

Chapter 17

A Good Night's Sleep

It had been almost one in the morning when Eleanor had finally fallen asleep, but she had nevertheless woken very early. Her concerns about the unicorn had made her anxious and unable to sleep in. She'd woken just before five and her first fretful thoughts were of the unicorn, but when she sat up, she found a note from Merrie propped up on her bedside table.

"Dear Princess Baby," it said in Merrie's big loopy writing. "Great news! As you requested, Hobbs took your you-know-what back to Swinley F. in the wee small hours. He later called to confirm that your 'friend' had been successfully returned to his forest and had already begun to recover. You were absolutely right to send him home. Clever girl. Well done! See you soon. Yours as always, Merrie xoxoxo."

Merrie was right. It was great news—the greatest. Eleanor felt so relieved and happy the unicorn was home that she didn't want to go back to sleep. Instead she wrapped herself in her quilt and sat on her window seat, gazing out at the strangely quiet city.

She had never been up so early or seen the streets in front of the palace so empty and quiet. There were no tourists sitting on the steps of the Victoria Memorial, the large white monument that stood in front of the palace. There were no sightseers clinging to the railings or pestering the red-coated guards. There were no cars, no taxis, no tour buses—nothing. There was only a magical, empty stillness.

Except, she realized, not everything was still. She was staring at the golden angel on top of the Victoria Memorial, when she thought she saw something small moving on the top of one of the ornate lampposts nearby. It was something she could only see out of the corner of her eye, because when she turned to look, whatever it was wasn't there. At first she'd thought that it must have been a bird, but there was no bird on the lamppost. She gazed at the angel some more and could again see the tiny, shadowy movements. This time she could see some more movements on her left side, but again only out of the corners of her eyes. It was very frustrating. Eleanor felt sure it was a fairy. If only she could find a way to see them clearly.

Now her thoughts scrambled back to the day of the hunt, when she'd seen that one by the woods. What had been so different about that day? Why had she been able to see a fairy then, but not now? What had she been doing? And what about the time she'd seen the two winged maids on the chandelier and the footman on the dining table?

Did it, she wondered, have to do with her frame of mind? She'd been happy that day in the woods. It had been lovely just lying in the long grass daydreaming. And the time she'd seen the footman on the table, she'd been excited because she'd been promised she could see her parents before the grand banquet— unfortunately in the end that hadn't happened— and she'd been daydreaming about how nice that would be.

She couldn't remember exactly how she'd been feeling when she'd seen the maids on the chandelier. She recalled she'd just been lying in her bed staring at nothing in particular, lost in her thoughts. She'd been daydreaming.

Eleanor sat up. Was that what it took to see a fairy?

It was worth a try. She fixed her eyes on the angel and tried to daydream.

Twice she felt that she was really getting somewhere, but each time, the moment she consciously thought about the movements or tried to look at them directly, they instantly vanished. Seeing fairies began to feel as tricky as catching fish with your hands, but Eleanor knew even that was possible.

She took a deep breath and stared at the angel, allowing her eyes to relax. Soon her mind drifted off. When she noticed the fluttering in the corners of her eyes, she ignored it and turned her thoughts away. She was happily daydreaming about this and that when she suddenly remembered the unicorn. Thank goodness he was back in his forest! She smiled when she recalled that Hobbs had told Merrie that the unicorn was already getting better. Maybe his coat was pure white and his horn and hooves were gold again. She would miss him, but she could always see him whenever they stayed at Swinley Castle.

It was as she thought these happy thoughts that the world outside her window seemed to snap into focus. Eleanor gasped. Now she could see them as clearly as she could see the palace railings or the guards by the gates. In a split second she had acquired the knack. Princess Eleanor could see the fairies!

She looked this way and that, and this time they didn't disappear when she turned to look at them directly. There was the one on top of the lamppost—he was exercising—bouncing up and down doing jumping jacks, then running in place. Two more fairies stood at the foot of the monument talking. A lone black cab motored up the Mall and the princess saw fairies riding on the top. Then she looked at the trees and almost fell off her seat. The trees were teeming with fairies. Eleanor laughed out loud. She had never imagined that the world would be so full of them.

As the city awoke and more cars began to drive along the Mall, Princess Eleanor started noticing more and more fairies. Before long, the skies were full of smartly dressed ones whizzing hither and thither. It was incredible that all this must have been going on around her every day, but she'd never seen it before. There were even, she noticed, fairy guards in smart uniforms stationed above the human ones at the palace gates.

The guards reminded her of the maid fairies and the footman she'd seen inside the palace long ago. Perhaps one of those palace fairies would talk to her. She spun around and quickly scanned the room. Now that she had the knack she spotted the fairy footman almost immediately.

He was dressed just like the one she'd seen polishing the glasses years ago. He wore a smart green jacket, black knickerbockers, long white socks, and neat black shoes.

Eleanor jumped up and ran across the room. "Excuse me, sir?" she asked clearly and politely. "Would you come and talk with me for a minute, please? I want to know all about you. Hello?"

The fairy footman glanced down at her, but when he realized she was addressing him, he shrieked and fled through an opening in the elaborate plaster cornice.

Eleanor would have tried to coax him out, but Merrie walked in just at that moment. The princess would have to postpone her fairy fun till later on.

"Good morning, Princess Baby," chirruped Merrie brightly. She was smiling, but she had dark circles under her eyes. "Did you get my note?"

"Yes, Merrie," replied the princess. "Thank you for having Hobbs do what I wanted. I'm so happy the unicorn is back where he belongs."

"Wonderful," said Merrie as she strode into the bathroom and turned the taps on full blast. "We've got a lot to do today," she said as she came out of the bathroom and disappeared into the princess's wardrobe. "First, after breakfast, we have an hour of Latin scheduled, then just for fun some good old-fashioned arithmetic."

"Wonderful!" said Eleanor, distracted by the changing of the fairy guard that was taking place outside her window. It was similar to the human changing of the guard except that the fairy one took place ten feet above the top of the railings and involved some very fancy flying.

"Your Highness?" said Merrie.

"Sorry, Merrie." Eleanor beamed at her governess and danced her way to the bathroom. She was so happy she didn't mind an hour of Latin after breakfast, or two hours of arithmetic after that. She could see fairies and the unicorn was safe in his forest. She didn't mind anything at all.

There was much unhappiness in the palace fairy servants' hall when second fairy footman Ashley Hanson reported how the princess had tried to speak to him. The palace fairy butler, Mr. Yeats, a neat, precise, and extremely elegant fairy, was deeply perturbed by this news. He paced in front of the miserable footman while the senior members of the palace fairy staff stood by, waiting to see what he would do.

"How did this happen?" Yeats asked, speaking

more to himself than the distraught Hanson. "The princess has never noticed any of our fairy staff before. Well, not since she was in her crib."

"Should I let Mr. Cedric and Mr. Anatole know, sir?" asked one of the upper fairy maids.

Mr. Yeats nodded. "Yes, advise them to keep a close eye—dash it! It's their day off today. See if you can get ahold of them, Dawkins, warn them of the situation." Mr. Yeats looked sternly around at the servants. "You must all keep as low a profile as possible. No flitting about when the princess is present—she'll be on the lookout for us now. We have to be extremely careful." Mr. Yeats's face paled. "Not a word to anyone about this," he said in a choked voice. "If the castle fairies find out, William Butler will never, ever let me forget it."

As she'd slept beneath the pile of yellow petals, Joyce had dreamed of the unicorn. He was running through the forest and she was following. She couldn't see him properly. Every time she got close enough, something spooked him and off he went again. She only caught a flash of a hoof or the swish of his tail, but she could hear him whinnying as though he was in pain. Joyce wanted to help him, but he wouldn't let her reach him. He ran on and on, crashing through the trees, cutting himself on the sharp branches. Joyce was flying as fast as she could, but she couldn't catch up.

Joyce woke in a panic and found herself looking at the sky through a straggly bush dotted with yellow flowers. It felt early. The air was cool and the sky was light, though only just; the sun was not yet above the horizon. She could hear a dull, constant roar coming from somewhere close by.

Yellow petals tumbled down as she sat up slowly. She was afraid that moving her injured wing would be unbearably painful, but she had to try. Gingerly, she stretched it out and to her amazement found it didn't hurt at all. She stood up and opened her wings all the way and flapped them. It was incredible. When she'd fallen asleep she'd felt a hundred years old. Now she felt as good as new.

Joyce was mystified until she realized the bush with the yellow flowers was Saint-John's-wort. Her mother always used that herb in poultices to heal sprains and bruises. That was why she felt so good. Those miraculous yellow petals had healed her wing while she slept.

"Thank you," she said to the bush. "Now, if only you could tell me how to get to London."

She looped her bag across her body and took off.

Once she was above the carpet of wildflowers, she paused and hovered, not knowing which way to go. Now she had no map, no compass, nor any stars to guide her.

She turned in the air. In one direction the ground sloped down and disappeared beneath the mists of the grim moor. Not that way for sure. In the opposite direction the ground sloped up to the top of a grassy hill, above which, she noticed, was the brightest part of the morning sky.

Sunrise! Of course, the sun rose in the east and London was east of where she'd been. Joyce nodded to herself and flew up the hill. At least for a little while she would know where east lay, but sound though this plan was, it very soon transpired that she didn't need it at all.

As she flew up the hill, the incessant roaring she had heard upon waking grew louder and louder. It wasn't a pleasant sound.

When she reached the top of the hill, the full force of the noise hit her. Hundreds of cars and trucks and buses were charging along the motorway that was at the bottom of the other side of the hill.

It was a shock. She'd been expecting to see more countryside, not this busy, noisy road so close that the wind from the trucks blasted her back. She quickly took cover in the lee of the hill and sat down to think. She had seen something beyond the road. Something in the distance. Something that she couldn't quite believe was real.

Bravely she poked her head above the brow of the hill for another look. What she saw took her breath away.

Beyond the road, the land dipped down slowly like the side of a shallow bowl. It was a bowl that was miles wide and every square inch of it seemed to be covered with buildings of all sorts of shapes and sizes. At the edge closest to the road were row after row of houses like the ones she'd seen in Wheatby. There were bigger buildings, too, arranged in haphazard clusters and dotted about all over the endless urban sprawl. There were roads and bridges, there were chimneys belching smoke, and far in the distance there was an enormous cluster of even taller buildings, silhouetted by the sun just now rising behind them. A town this large, with so many buildings, had to be a city, Joyce was sure of it.

She held her breath, trying not to get too excited before she'd thought this through. She knew there were no cities between Swinley and London, so this meant that either she'd gone horribly astray and stumbled upon some other city in England, or that she was now looking at London.

The great gray road in front of her headed straight toward the city. Farther along the road there was a big blue sign on a metal arch above the traffic. Joyce narrowed her eyes and strained to read it. She could just make out the words LONDON CITY CENTRE 3m. Three miles.

Suddenly everything seemed possible. London was so close. She would fly there, find the palace, and somehow she would take the unicorn home to the forest.

With one strenuous flap of her wings, she soared into the sky, then, when she was sure she was above the wind from the traffic, she turned toward the city. She would, she felt sure, be with the unicorn soon.

For the first part of the morning Princess Eleanor hadn't been paying that much attention to her governess and hadn't really noticed her odd behavior. Not only were her thoughts full of happiness knowing that she had done the right thing in returning the unicorn to the forest, but also her newly rediscovered ability to see fairies made it extremely difficult to pay attention to her schoolwork. Every time she glanced through the window and saw so many fairies flitting along the Mall, she felt a great rush of excitement.

The princess might never have noticed Merrie's strange behavior if it hadn't been for the almost constant beeping of her cell phone. Princess Eleanor soon began to wonder what was going on.

Merrie was definitely not herself today. She seemed on edge. She jumped whenever Eleanor spoke to her. Staring at her computer screen, she ground her teeth and clenched her jaw, and when she typed, which she did in rapid bursts, she giggled and bashed at the keys like a maniac. Her eyes flashed as she leafed back and forth through a thick, messy notepad Eleanor had never seen her use before. She muttered to herself as she ticked things off or scribbled notes on the pad. Strangest of all, she kept trotting to the bathroom every five minutes and staying in there for ages. Something was definitely up.

Merrie was also more dressed up than usual, as though she'd made a special effort. Her usual plain black dress was not black, but a very dark purple. It was the one Merrie only wore on special occasions. She was also wearing her special two strings of pearls with matching earrings, and shoes with heels rather than her usual sensible flats. Eleanor noticed that she'd taken more care with her makeup, too. Pale violet eye shadow and thick black mascara, a stripe of blusher on each cheek, and red lipstick a shade brighter than usual. Her hair, which had been set and curled and lacquered into a coppery cotton candy construction, was bigger than Eleanor had ever seen it.

Eleanor wondered if Merrie had a boyfriend. That might explain the giggling.

After breakfast Merrie had told Eleanor to study on her own, but that hadn't worked well. Latin grammar was one of the very few subjects in which the princess did not excel, and instead of studying she'd needed many things explained. It soon became obvious that Merrie didn't want to be bothered with answering her questions.

"Very well," Merrie announced after Eleanor had interrupted her again. "Put your grammar books away. I think it's time for some sustained silent reading."

Eleanor was shocked. Merrie was telling her to read? Merrie never let her read during schooltime. Reading for reading's sake was, according to Merrie, a ridiculous waste of time. Merrie didn't even object when Eleanor chose to read a novel. Normally Merrie strongly disapproved of fiction, but this morning she didn't say a thing.

It was really very strange.

Chapter 18

A Way In

On hot summer days the lunchtime crush in Soho, London, is a wonderful sight. People spill out of their office buildings and spread themselves on any available bit of grass. They stand outside pubs, glasses of wine and pints of beer in hand. The tables outside restaurants fill up rapidly, and swivel-hipped waiters swerve between them bringing baskets of bread and saucers of olive oil and balsamic vinegar to the customers. The women wear bright summer dresses and high-heeled sandals and the men take off their jackets and roll up their sleeves. Everybody smiles.

Joyce flew above it all. She flew above the red

buses and the black-backed taxis, above the waiters and the picnickers in the parks, above the tourists in the sightseeing boats on the river, and above the London Zoo, which was packed with hot and sticky visitors.

To her the city seemed a bewilderingly busy place. Fairies were packed onto the roofs of buses while others rode in style alone on the tops of cars and taxicabs. The air was crowded with hundreds, no, thousands of them, all hurrying in every direction as though there was no tomorrow. One or two were moving so fast that they bashed into her, but no one said sorry. One even scolded her for being in the way.

At street level the pavements were crammed with big people, all apparently caught in the same crazy mad dash as the fairies. The city, Joyce soon realized, was a mad place.

It was almost noon and the day was blisteringly hot. Joyce was getting tired, but she still hadn't found Buckingham Palace. She knew she would have to ask someone for help but she hated the idea. She didn't want a repeat of her experience in Wheatby. Still, she had to try. Hopefully these fairies would be more understanding.

"Excuse me," she asked a fairy who was hurrying by. "Could you tell me which way it is to—"

"Can't help you," replied the fairy, cutting her off as he whizzed by. "No time. Important things to do."

"Oh," said Joyce. She tried again.

A large fairy with a good number of shopping bags bustled toward her.

"Excuse me," Joyce began, but the large fairy suddenly cried out, "Oh, my bus!" and, bags rustling, wings flapping, she made a beeline for the top of a number three bus. Once there she waved back at Joyce.

"Sorry, dear," she shouted. "If I'd missed this, I'd be waiting for another all afternoon."

She wasn't mean, at least, thought Joyce.

The crowds seemed to be getting worse, and to get away Joyce flew down a street to the right and soon found herself in a large shady square with a park in the center. The trees in the park were almost as tall as the buildings, which meant that nearly the whole square was dappled with a lovely cool shade. It was a relief to be out of the glare of the sun.

In the middle of the square was a small black and white hut that looked like a little shop. There were racks of postcards and souvenirs, a counter with candy, and a cooler full of bottles and cans. The shopkeeper sat on a stool beside the shop. Her dog, a Jack Russell, lay panting in a basket at her feet.

Joyce hadn't had anything to eat since she'd sat on Millets Mountain and she was horribly hungry. She was also badly in need of a drink, but she had no water left. The cans and bottles in the cooler at the shop were packed in ice. A piece of that would quench her thirst.

As soon as Joyce landed on the lip of the cooler, the dog jumped to his feet.

"Yap yap yap!" he barked, bouncing up and down. Joyce grabbed an ice cube in both hands and flew out of reach.

"Quiet, Kiki!" said the woman, swatting the dog on the head with a rolled-up newspaper. Kiki whimpered and shot back in her basket.

Joyce sat on the lowest rung of the postcard rack and sucked on the ice cube. Where on earth was that palace? She couldn't come this far and fail. She had to find the unicorn. But how? Her mind was racing, but she wasn't getting anywhere. Then she remembered something Sam used to say.

"Best thing to do when you're in a hurry is to slow it down. Slow it down till you can think clearly. Take a nice deep breath, then blow it out and relax. Nine times out of ten the answer will just fall into your lap."

"Slow it down," she told herself now. "Slow it down." She breathed in, then let her breath out as slowly as she could and felt herself grow calmer. She wondered if the solution to her problem would just fall into her lap. She looked up, half expecting to see an answer already falling down toward her, but it wasn't falling, it was stuck in the rack right above her head! Joyce gasped. It couldn't be. No, surely not. Was is that simple? She flew off her perch and turned to face the postcard rack. It was!

There was her answer. A postcard with a beautiful, brightly illustrated map of central London on it. It had been right in front of her, or rather right behind her, all along.

Joyce quickly found the square where she was, then she searched for the palace. There it was, and it was close, no more than five or six fairy miles as the fairy flew. If she flew at top speed, she'd be there in no time.

At eleven thirty Merrie emerged from the princess's bathroom. She had her purple cell phone in her hand and was smiling gleefully. When she noticed the princess looking at her, she dropped the smile and put her phone away.

"Time to get ready, Princess Baby," she announced brightly as she quickly closed her laptop and locked it away in her desk drawer. "Come along, my love," she said, dropping the drawer key in her purse. "You're opening the new children's dinosaur exhibit at the museum at twelve thirty. Here's your coat, my love."

She held out the princess's pink jacket and shook it at the princess like a bullfighter shakes his cape at a bull. Still puzzling over Merrie's giddiness, Princess Eleanor put her book away and slipped her arms in the jacket's sleeves, then followed her governess outside.

The car was waiting at the entrance for Princess Eleanor and Merrie. It was Captain Simperington's day off and the relief Royal bodyguard, Lieutenant Philip Robinson, respectfully held open the rear door. Eleanor hesitated on the step. There were fairy guards standing on the roof of the Royal car—three uniformed ones at the back and three at the front. Eleanor couldn't believe it—fairy security! She glanced at her governess and her bodyguard, but neither of them seemed to have noticed a thing.

"Princess Baby?" prompted Merrie, prodding Eleanor in the small of her back. Eleanor obediently got into the car, followed by Merrie. Lieutenant Robinson made sure the door was closed, then got in beside the chauffeur.

As the car set off, Merrie was once again jabbing at

the keys on her cell phone. Merrie's sending more text messages? thought Eleanor. What on earth is going on?

When the car pulled out of the palace courtyard, Eleanor forgot all about Merrie and her odd behavior. The princess almost screamed when she saw the crowd of fairies gathered at the palace railings. There were now as many fairies as there were tourists. And there seemed to be just as many different nationalities as well.

Setting her cheek against the glass, Eleanor tilted her head back to look up at the fairies as the car passed through the gate. She had always found London a fascinating city, but now that she could see all the fairies it was even more so. She couldn't stop watching them. Hundreds of fairies were going about their business in the trees, and on the road large groups of them were riding on the roofs of cars and taxis. Some were even riding on people's backs.

The museum was full of fairies as well. Parties of school-age fairies were tearing through the dinosaur hall. Some were even climbing on the dinosaur skeletons until a fat fairy in a museum guard's uniform flew over and shouted at them to get off.

It wasn't easy to concentrate on opening the new

children's dinosaur exhibit. She kept forgetting what she was supposed to say. She kept drifting off and staring all agog at the fairies flitting across the beautiful vaulted ceiling. Merrie had to prompt her more than once.

After the opening ceremony was over, Merrie hustled Eleanor out to the car and within moments they were on their way back to the palace.

Joyce flew swiftly down the Mall. Once she knew the way to go, it hadn't been too difficult to find this beautiful, wide, tree-lined street with a park on one side and magnificent peach-colored buildings on the other. Placed high on every lamppost a double bracket, angled like the hands of a clock at ten to two, held a pair of vibrant flags, one on either side. Far ahead, honey-colored and stately, Buckingham Palace could be seen through the trees. No flag flew from the mast on the palace roof. Their Majesties were not in residence. They had left that morning on a state visit to Denmark.

When Joyce reached the palace, she saw that getting in was not going to be easy. A huge crowd of humans stood peering through the black and gold railings. Red-coated Royal horse guards stood smartly to attention at the palace gates and stopped anyone from entering. The soldiers looked uncomfortably hot in their thick bearskin helmets.

Hundreds of fairies hovered in the air, many of them holding on to the railings' golden fleurs-de-lis. A line of palace fairy guards resplendent with their own red uniforms and glittering silver wings warned the crowds of fairies to stay back.

Joyce soon saw why the fairies never flew beyond the top of the railings. A fairy child who was holding a balloon let go of the string. The instant she tried to chase after it platoons of fairy guards flew in from nowhere and surrounded her. The young fairy's mother was furious with the guards for scaring the child. The guards looked sheepish and ashamed. One of them even flew off and retrieved the balloon.

Joyce flew to the big white monument in front of the palace and landed on the top of the golden angel's head. She stared down at the cars whizzing around the roundabout and tried to think of a way to get inside the palace. Nothing came to her until she saw the gates of the palace swing open to let a car go out. Joyce smiled. If cars came out of the palace, they must also go in. Perhaps she could get in that way. Now all she needed was to find a car going to the palace.

Watching both the gates and the cars on the road,

Joyce waited for her chance. It wasn't long before it came. The next time the gates opened there was no car waiting to leave. Joyce leapt into the air and spotted a black limousine speeding down the Mall toward the palace. She set off and zoomed toward it.

As the car drew nearer, she saw it was astonishingly well guarded. Three fairy guards rode at the rear of the roof and three at the front. She'd never get on the car without being spotted. Then she noticed that the limo's right-side rear window was open just a fraction. It might just be wide enough for her to slip through.

Joyce hovered in midair and waited . . . waited . . . waited . . . then, when the moment felt exactly right, she shot off, wings a blur, toward the car.

She was almost at the window when she knew she'd misjudged it. Her angle was slightly off. She wasn't going to make it through the gap. She quickly made an adjustment to her wing speed, and though it wasn't enough to get her through the opening it enabled her to catch hold of the edge of the window. Unfortunately her arms weren't strong enough to pull herself up so she could climb in.

Her arms ached and she would probably have soon let go, had not the limousine at that very moment fortuitously driven over one of London's famous cast-iron manhole covers, which, being beautifully embossed with the Royal Coat of Arms, made the car bounce just enough to cause Joyce to be lifted up and flung through the window.

She shot into the back of the limousine and landed unnoticed and unharmed in a sea of soft, frilly pink fabric that was spread over the backseat.

Joyce soon saw that the pink frills belonged to the skirt of a girl who was intently watching something out of the window. Joyce pushed the frills out of her way and sat up. She glanced at the other occupant of the backseat. It was that bony woman, the one with the copper-colored hair, the one she'd seen with . . .

Joyce stopped. Did that mean . . . ? Openmouthed, she turned and stared up at the girl at the window. Was that her? Was that the princess? Was that the one who had taken the unicorn away? Joyce didn't have to wait long to find out.

As the car raced quickly into the palace courtyard, the copper-haired woman tapped the girl on the leg. "Princess Baby?" she said with a sugary smile. "We have to get out now."

Princess Baby? thought Joyce. Yes, that was her. Suddenly Joyce gasped. Oh no! The princess could see her! She would have to hide, and fast.

A pink jacket with frills around the collar and cuffs

lay on the seat between the princess and the woman. Joyce saw it had a little pocket. She ran for it and dived in, just a microsecond before the princess picked up the jacket and slipped it on.

Joyce landed in the bottom of the pocket amidst a jumble of sticky candy wrappers and bits of fluff.

What, she wondered, am I going to do now?

The princess's limousine drew up at the porticoed entrance, and a footman in a plain, dark suit trotted down the steps to open the car door. Merrie couldn't wait that long. She opened her own door, got out, and shot up the steps.

As Princess Eleanor got out of the car, she happened to glance back toward the stable entrance and was surprised to see a man who looked very like Hobbs heading inside.

"Simpers?" she asked, without taking her eyes off the man by the stables. "Is that—"

"Ahem, I'm afraid you've got me today, Your Highness," said Lieutenant Robinson respectfully. "How may I be of service?"

The princess blinked up at the tall, slim lieutenant. "Oh—oh," she stammered. "Sorry, Robbo, I forgot it was Simpers's day off. It's nothing important, thank you."

Eleanor looked back at the stable, but there was now no sign of the man she'd thought was Hobbs.

"Lessons, Your Highness!" said Merrie, who was waiting for her by the door.

"Coming, Merrie," replied the princess. The lieutenant escorted her to the top of the steps. Merrie eyed him coldly.

"That's all, Lieutenant Robinson, " she said snottily. "The princess will not be leaving the palace again today."

The lieutenant turned to the princess and bowed respectfully.

"Thank you, Robbo," said Eleanor, before following Merrie inside.

When they reached the study, Merrie told Eleanor to go on with her reading. The princess opened her book but she couldn't concentrate on it. She kept thinking about the man she'd seen at the stables. Hobbs was supposed to have stayed with the unicorn at Swinley. Why would he have come back?

"Merrie?" she asked.

Merrie's head shot up from the notepad she'd been scowling at. "What? I'm sorry." She checked herself and plastered a smile on her face. "Yes, my sweet?"

"Hobbs didn't come back from Swinley, did he?" asked Eleanor.

Merrie's smile froze. "Why, no, my dear," she replied, speaking slowly. "Why would you think he had?"

"I thought I saw him at the stable entrance just now."

Merrie shook her head and sighed impatiently. "I don't think so, Your Highness. It was probably one of the other grooms," she added, ripping a few pages from the notepad. "One scruffy, tweedy serf looks pretty much like the next, doesn't he?"

Eleanor wasn't convinced. "Do you think you could just telephone the stables and see if—"

"No, I can't," snapped Merrie. "I don't have time. Now get on with your book and stop pestering me."

The princess was shocked. Merrie had never before talked to her like that. Merrie was often bossy, but she was never rude. She didn't snap. But Merrie looked different today—as different as she'd looked sneaking down the corridor at midnight. She looked mean and small as she fed the torn pages from her notepad into the shredder beside her desk.

Then Merrie's behavior became even more erratic. She kept starting various tasks, but she couldn't settle to anything. One minute she was pulling dead petals off the flowers on the table, the next she was at the window chewing her lip, the next she was hunting for something in her purse, the next she was across the room straightening the books on the shelves, and every few seconds she checked her watch and then her phone. She rooted in her purse and found the small key to her desk drawer. She was just taking out her laptop when her phone beeped.

Merrie jumped up with a little squeak. She put her laptop on the desk, snatched up the phone, and flipped it open. Eleanor studied Merrie's face as she read the message. The governess's eyes were as bright as two wet pebbles and she was grinning like a schoolgirl. She snapped the phone shut, then turned to Eleanor and smiled an ingratiating smile.

"Now then, Your HIGHness, Princess Bay-BEE," she sniggered. "I have to go out. You stay here and read your nice booky wook. Okeydokey?"

Merrie trotted to the mirror and, leaning in close, quickly reapplied her lipstick and smoothed down her eyebrows, then she stood back to admire her reflection.

"Hobbs did take the unicorn back to the forest, didn't he?" asked the princess, intently watching Merrie's face.

Merrie stopped admiring herself and regarded Eleanor in the mirror. For an instant there was a flicker of something unreadable in her eyes. "Of course he did," she said. Eleanor wanted to ask her more, but Merrie was already collecting her things. She grabbed her purse and her gloves, then she rudely shot past Eleanor and ran across the room.

"Must dash," she said, opening the door with a flourish and grinning back at Eleanor. "Work hard. Back soon! Ta-ta!" Then she left, slamming the door shut behind her.

After Merrie had gone, Princess Eleanor sat at her school desk and tried to think clearly. It bothered her that Merrie had been so quick to dismiss the idea that it was Hobbs she'd seen by the stables. Merrie hadn't seen the man; she didn't know. The grooms didn't all look alike. Only Hobbs looked like Hobbs. Eleanor was almost certain it had been him.

There was only one way to find out. She would go and see if she could find him. She hurried to the door, listened to make sure Merrie had gone, and turned the handle and pulled, but the door did not budge. It was locked.

"No!" gasped Eleanor, trying the door again and again. It still wouldn't budge. She gave up and ran through the adjoining door to her bedroom, where she tried the other door to the corridor, but that too was locked. Eleanor could not believe it. Merrie had locked her in! She banged on her bedroom door and shouted for help at the top of her voice, but no one came.

She tried the telephone, but the line was dead. The cable had been cut. It was the same with the other phones. She tried the servants' bell, but the cord came away in her hand. She ran to the windows and looked out, hoping that one of the guards might see her, but they were all facing out from the palace and propriety stopped her from waving her arms to attract the attention of the tourists at the gates.

Why would Merrie lock me in? thought Eleanor. But she obviously had.

Eleanor frowned and realized that Merrie's strange behavior had begun when they'd first seen the unicorn in Swinley Forest. She took a deep breath and thought back carefully over the last few days. She remembered how Merrie, who had never cared for horses, had been so keen for her to take the unicorn home. She recalled how when they'd first brought the unicorn to the palace Merrie had been eager for her to spend time with him, even letting her off lessons early so that she could go to the stables. But all that had changed yesterday after her morning visit to the stables. After that Merrie had kept her busy with schoolwork, and then had insisted that she keep

appointments that could have easily been postponed—
the dress fitting, the portrait sitting, the cookie bak-
ing. It was almost as if Merrie hadn't wanted her to go
near the stables. And then there'd been the unex-
pected and irresistible outing to the theater—never
before had Merrie sprung such a spontaneous treat on
her. Had Merrie arranged that just to keep her away
from the unicorn?

The princess gasped—what about the missing
shoes! Had Merrie sent all her shoes to be cleaned to
stop her from sneaking to the stables on her own?

Eleanor's thoughts raced. She tried to think posi-
tively of her governess. Perhaps Merrie had known
how sick the unicorn had become; perhaps she was
just trying to protect the princess from seeing him that
way. Was that it? But then Eleanor remembered seeing Hobbs by the stables and she recalled the look
she'd seen in Merrie's eye when she'd asked her if
he'd really taken the unicorn back.

"No!" she cried. "NO!" She clutched one of the
bedposts and pressed her forehead against the wood.
"Merrie wouldn't lie to me!" she whispered, but her
eyes were already full of tears. All the evidence
pointed the other way. "No!" she cried, throwing herself across the pink counterpane. "No! No! NO!"

Eleanor landed on the bed with such force that Joyce, who all this time had been trying to think of a way she could escape unseen, was thrown from the princess's pocket and sent reeling through the air. She landed on the counterpane, right beside the princess's enormous tear-splotched face.

"I didn't mean to do it!" the princess cried with her eyes shut tight. "I didn't mean for him to get sick! I didn't even want to take him. I wish I'd never . . . I wish I'd never . . . seen that fairy." Then she opened her eyes and saw Joyce right there on the counterpane.

"YOU!" she cried.

"M-me?" stammered Joyce.

"Yes, you!"

Joyce tried to fly away but Eleanor was too quick. She caught her in both hands.

"Let me go!" protested Joyce, struggling to get out of the princess's grip.

"No!" replied the princess, scooting to the edge of the bed. She held Joyce out in front of her. "This . . . this . . . whole mess . . . it's all your fault!"

"What?" retorted Joyce defensively. "No, it isn't. You were the one who took the unicorn."

"Yes, but I wouldn't have seen him," continued

the princess, "if you hadn't been fluttering in front of my nose, would I?"

"I couldn't help it," Joyce protested. "I fell out of the tree when you sneezed!"

"Even so," the princess went on, "if you'd come back when I called you—"

"I was scared!" Joyce explained. "You're a lot bigger than me!"

But the princess was no longer listening. She seemed to be talking to herself.

"—but you didn't come back—so I ran after you and . . . and then . . . and then I saw him. . . ." She suddenly stopped and blinked. Her lip trembled and a fat tear rolled slowly down her cheek. "I should never have taken him," she whispered.

"Then why did you?" cried Joyce in an exasperated voice.

"He was so lovely," Eleanor replied, "and he seemed to want to stay with me so much, and then Merrie, my governess, suggested that we take him home—"

"Yes, I remember," said Joyce. "But you didn't have to listen to her. You could have said no! You're supposed to be a princess, aren't you?"

"Yes." Eleanor nodded, then she frowned slightly

and set Joyce gently down on the bedside table. "It's just that sometimes I don't feel much like one."

"Well, maybe if you acted more like one, you would," retorted Joyce.

She instantly regretted what she'd said. Princess Eleanor looked stunned, as though Joyce had slapped her hard.

The princess just stared at her, moving her lips as though she wanted to say something but couldn't find the words. Then suddenly, she hung her head and burst into tears.

Joyce felt awful. She flew to the princess, pushed through the screen of blond curls, and, doing her best to dodge the teardrops, she hovered in front of Eleanor's face.

"Please don't cry," she said kindly. "Please. I'm sorry. You were right, it was all my fault." The princess shook her head and her tears fell faster.

Joyce pushed back through the hair and flew to a box of tissues on the dresser. "Come on, it's not that bad," she said, returning with a pink tissue for the princess.

"It is!" sobbed the princess. Then between sniffles Eleanor quickly told Joyce everything that had happened since they'd brought the unicorn to London. When she told her how ill he'd become, Joyce listened quietly without interrupting until Eleanor got to the part about how she'd asked Merrie to have the unicorn taken back to the forest.

"Well, that's all right then," cried Joyce, feeling relieved. "That's fantastic. You did exactly the right thing by sending him home. He was sick because no unicorn can survive for long outside his forest, in the same way his forest can't survive without him. That's why I've come to find him and take him home. But if he's already back there then everything's going to be all r—hey? Hey? No need for more tears."

The princess shook her head vehemently. "It's just that . . . Oh . . . I don't think he's really back there at all . . . I think . . . I think . . . Merrie lied to me . . . I don't know why . . . but I'm sure she did . . . I think he's still here . . . in the stables . . . and if he is . . . he must be really sick."

Joyce felt cold inside. If the princess's suspicions were right, they had to get to the unicorn as soon as possible. Eleanor blew her nose fiercely. Joyce held on to a lock of hair to stop herself from being blown away.

"No more crying," said Joyce gently when the princess had finished wiping her nose.

Eleanor nodded. "I'm sorry I got angry with you before," she said.

"And I'm sorry I snapped at you about the princess thing."

"That's all right." Eleanor shrugged. "I deserved it. Do you think . . . ? I mean . . . could we start over and be friends?"

"I'd like that very much," said Joyce, smiling.

"I don't even know your name."

"I'm Joyce," said Joyce.

"It's nice to meet you, Joyce. I'm Eleanor, or Princess Eleanor Charlotte Anya Ilona Grace Victoria if you want the whole kit and caboodle." Joyce raised her eyebrows and puffed out her cheeks. Eleanor made a face. "It is a bit of a mouthful, isn't it?"

The princess took a deep breath, then got up from the bed. "Right," she said, taking charge. "First we need to find out if the unicorn is still here. We can decide our best course of action once we know the facts. But we can't do anything until we get out of here."

Chapter 19

The Americans

Ten minutes later Joyce stood at one end of the princess's bedstead and leaned against the post with her arms folded, grimly watching Eleanor pace back and forth. They'd tried everything they could think of to get out of the princess's rooms, but nothing had worked.

The keyhole was too small for Joyce to squeeze through. The palace windows were too heavy for the princess to open so Joyce couldn't fly for help. And, as not one of the security cameras on the outside of the palace pointed toward the Royal windows—it would be an intrusion on the Royal Family's privacy—they couldn't attract the attention of any security guards, either human or fairy.

"There has to be someone who can help. What about that big man?" suggested Joyce. "The one who was with you in the forest?"

"Simpers? No." The princess shook her head. "It's his day off and I can't call him. Merrie's fixed the phones, remember?"

"Don't you have one of those little ones like she does?" asked Joyce.

"No, Merrie wouldn't let me have one," replied Eleanor. "She said cell phones were common and she only had one for emergen—oh, of course!" the princess gasped. "Merrie didn't want me calling my parents. She's always keeping me from 'bothering' them. It's always 'Be a good girl, Princess Baby, no, you can't see your parents.'" The princess's eyes shone with an angry fire. "No, Princess Baby, they have to see the king of Estonia or the queen of Lapland or the arch-rotten-bishop of Canterbury. They don't have a moment to come and say good night. . . ."

The princess's voice trailed off and a look of such heartbreaking sadness crossed over her face that Joyce felt tears come into her own eyes.

Joyce was desperately trying to think of a way she

could make herself as thin as a key when the princess suddenly cried out and ran to Merrie's desk.

"It's Merrie's laptop! Her computer!" gasped the princess, opening the slim black box that lay on the desk. "She was so distracted she must have forgotten to lock it away." The computer screen lit up, revealing pictures of some big fancy house on an Internet site. "I'll bet this will tell us what she's been up to." The princess went carefully through the list of Web sites that Merrie had recently visited. It was a long list, but none of them looked as though they had much to do with unicorns. In the past few days Merrie had visited a great number of real estate sites, discount travel sites, luxury yacht sites, some institute site, and a large number of online stores.

"Hold on—" said the princess, returning to click on the institute's site. She was quiet for a moment, and then she glanced up at Joyce. "Look at this," she said.

Joyce flew to her shoulder and peered at a bright blue Web page with an official-looking logo—a white circle with the letters "J.J.R." in blue across the middle.

" 'The J. J. Rosenthal Institute,' " Joyce read aloud, " 'dedicated to the academic pursuit of all things paranormal.' What does that mean?"

"That they'd be extremely interested in a real unicorn," replied the princess. She navigated swiftly around the institute's Web site and had just clicked on the word "reward" when Joyce suddenly shouted.

"Princess Eleanor, look!" she cried, pointing out of the window. "That's them, isn't it?"

Eleanor looked out of the window and saw Merrie leading three tall men toward the stables. Each one wore a short blue jacket with the J.J.R. logo across the back.

Eleanor grew pale. "Oh, Joyce, she must have brought them here. They'll hurt him. They'll test him and take clippings from his coat and analyze his blood."

"Why?" cried Joyce.

"To prove that he's real," replied the princess, brushing a tear from her cheek. "To prove that unicorns exist. The worst thing is that they won't care if he's sick, they won't even care if he dies. They'll just want to prove he's real. We have to stop them."

"Yes, we must!" agreed Joyce. "But how?" She flew to the window. Merrie and the experts had disappeared inside the stables. "Think, Joycey, think," she said aloud, trying to calm herself. "Come on. Think. Don't panic. Panicking will only waste more time."

Princess Eleanor let out a little yelp. "Panic?

Joyce, that's it! Why didn't I think of it sooner? I'll use the panicker!"

Joyce had no idea what the princess was talking about. She watched, bewildered, as Eleanor ran to the bed, then half disappeared beneath it. Joyce flew over and landed beside her.

"It's a panic button," said the princess, her voice muffled. "Simpers had it put under here in case kidnappers or robbers ever broke into my room. He said I just had to jump under the bed and press this button, and wherever he was he would come and rescue me. Here it is."

Joyce watched the princess press the small white button three times in quick succession. "That should do it!" she said, wriggling out from under the bed and dusting herself off. "Let's just hope Simps isn't too far away."

Captain Simperington was in the Odeon Cinema in Leicester Square about to take his seat for the afternoon showing of the latest blockbuster from the States. Simpers was extraordinarily fond of big, silly summer movies, and watching one on his own on the biggest cinema screen in London was his all-time favorite way of spending a free afternoon.

Moments before the princess pressed the panic

button, the well-built captain had been politely shuffling sideways down a crowded row, taking care not to stand on anybody's toes as he made his way to his seat. The house was dark because the preview trailers advertising the coming attractions had already begun.

Simpers carefully slotted his large drink into the drink holder, then began to lower himself into his seat, all the while trying not to spill popcorn over either of his neighbors. His behind was halfway down when the panic alarm suddenly went off on his cell phone.

AWHAAA—AWHAAA—AWHAAA!

His princess was in danger! Captain Simperington's reaction was instantaneous. He jackknifed up, flinging popcorn everywhere and knocking his drink all over his neighbor's lap. Without any apology, he charged back along the row, crushing toes and knees as he went. Angry shouts and complaints ensued, but Simpers didn't listen. His S.A.S. training had kicked in. He had one mission and only one—to save the princess.

He reached the aisle and dashed up it, and by the time the deep male voice in the trailer had finished saying the words "In a world where . . . ," Simpers was through the foyer and charging out into the bright light of day.

Back at the palace, Joyce and the princess were beginning to think he wasn't coming. They had been waiting for five full minutes.

"Where on earth can he be?" Eleanor fretted. "Oh, hurry up, Simpers, wherever you are!"

"Don't worry," said Joyce. "I'm sure that he and his friends will get here as soon as they can."

The princess raised her eyebrows. "His friends?" she asked.

"Yes. Well, I don't know if they're friends exactly," replied Joyce. "I mean those two scary-looking fairies that are always either on his shoulders or flying close by. Haven't you seen them?"

"You mean . . . are you saying Simpers can see fairies, too?" Eleanor asked, amazed. "That's incredible. I would never have guessed."

"It's odd that you never noticed his fairies when you can see me quite easily."

"I've only just relearned how to see any fairies at all. You were the first I'd been able to see in a very long time. Since then I've been practicing and getting better. Outside it's easier than here in the palace. I did see one by the cornice a couple of days ago, but he flew away the second he saw me watching him."

"Palace fairies!" Joyce shouted suddenly. "Of

course there must be palace fairies! We'll get *them* to help us." She leapt into the air and sped toward the ceiling. "I bet there's a door somewhere," she called down to Eleanor. "I'm going to go and find out!"

Chapter 20

Easy Money

Merrie opened the door of the stall and the three American experts from the institute filed in.

"You say it's in here?" said Professor Wursteinmunster, his unnaturally white teeth glinting in the gloom. "I can't see a thing."

Merrie waited till all three were inside the stall, then she shut the door and switched on the light.

In the middle of the stall stood Lemon, looking as much like an undersized pony and as little like a unicorn as it was possible to look.

"But, Cregg, that's just a horse," whined one of the other men.

"Not even," growled Wursteinmunster, white-lipped and furious. "More like a pony. A Shetland pony at that. If that's your unicorn, Ms. Merrieweather," he added in a tight voice, "I think we'd better leave. The institute's lawyers will be in touch, seeking compensation for our considerable expenses."

Merrie rolled her eyes. "For pity's sake, have a bit of patience, will you?" She leaned into the stall and bravely gave the princess's pony a good thwhack on the rump. Reluctantly Lemon shifted out of the way and the three men gasped as one. There at the back of the stall, lying in the hay, was the strangest horselike creature any of them had ever seen. Though its coat was dull and its hooves mottled, the horn on its forehead was unmistakable.

"Is that . . . ," gasped the professor, ". . . the unicorn?"

"Indeed it is," said Merrie. She folded her arms and rocked back on her heels. "Please have a good look."

Then, very quietly so as not to disturb this marvelous mythical creature, the three Americans moved closer and crouched respectfully in the damp, smelly straw.

In Princess Eleanor's bedchamber it didn't take Joyce long to find the fairy-sized door that was cleverly concealed in the plaster curls and spirals of the cornice.

Joyce turned and gave the thumbs-up signal to Eleanor, who was watching through a pair of opera glasses, or small binoculars. Joyce knocked on the door. It opened instantly and a fairy guard poked his head out. He looked Joyce up and down.

"Who are you?" he demanded in a not-very-friendly voice.

"I—I . . . ," stammered Joyce.

"Don't let him bully you, Joyce!" cried Eleanor from below. "Tell him we need their help to save the unicorn!"

The fairy guard's eyes nearly popped out of his head, and all the color left his face. He goggled at Joyce. "That isn't . . ." He gulped, quickly checking over his shoulder. He dropped his voice to a whisper. "Please, please tell me that wasn't . . . Princess Eleanor, was it?"

"Yes, it was," answered Joyce.

"Mr. Yeats!" The guard shrieked like a little girl and slammed the door shut.

"Come back, you coward!" shouted Joyce. "Come

back or I'm going to tell the castle fairies what wimps the palace fairies are!"

The door opened abruptly and a smart, gray-haired fairy in a natty dark suit stood there looking down at her.

Unnerved by his superior manner, Joyce automatically moved out of his way. The fairy flew through the door and stopped in midair. Three fairies followed him into the room—two were wearing the green velvet jackets and black knickerbockers of the palace fairy footmen, and the third, a tall, slim female fairy, wore a purple gown with a white collar and cuffs and her dark hair was fastened in an elegant chignon at the nape of her neck. She hovered beside the gray-haired fairy.

"Oh, Meester Yeats!" she whispered. "So it iz true. Ah, 'ow terrible. Her Highness can see us, no? I zink it must be ze fault of zis personne 'ere. No?" Madame Lardon nodded disdainfully at Joyce. Mr. Yeats glanced over, sniffed dismissively, and looked away. Joyce shivered.

The princess was getting impatient. "Hello!" she called. "Could you come and help me, please?"

The gray-haired fairy bowed his head graciously in response and then flew down, followed by his entourage. Joyce had never seen a fairy as elegant as this one. His long silver wings were more supple and exquisite than any that she'd ever seen back home in Swinley Hope, and yet he could fly fast and well on his.

On reaching the dressing table, Mr. Yeats slowed, held out his hand as a signal to the others, and then softly alighted beside a tall crystal jar full of pink cotton balls. The others landed behind him.

They all bowed deeply to the princess.

Joyce landed on the edge of the table close to Princess Eleanor. When they straightened up, the princess inclined her head regally to acknowledge them and Joyce, feeling she ought to do something too, curtseyed. The palace fairies looked at her dismissively. They did not bow back.

"Your Highness," said Mr. Yeats smoothly. "It is indeed our pleasure to attend you. How may we be of assistance?"

The princess narrowed her eyes at him, then lifted her chin slightly and straightened her back. It was a minor adjustment, but it made her seem much more of a princess and much less of a little girl.

"What is your name?" she asked.

"Yeats, Your Highness. I'm the fairy butl—"

"Well, Yeats," she said, interrupting him. "This fairy beside me is Joyce. She is my friend, and I expect you and your staff to treat her with the utmost respect or I shall want an explanation. Is that understood?" Her eyes glittered when she said this.

"Yes, Your Highness," said Mr. Yeats with a bow. Then he clicked his fingers at the other fairies and all of them, including Mr. Yeats, turned and bowed to Joyce. Joyce's face flushed red.

The princess nodded. "Now, to business. Mr. Yeats, can you get us out of here? The door's locked, and we need to get to the stables right away."

"Of course, Your Highness," replied the butler. He nodded to the two fairy footmen behind him, and they immediately set to work. They picked up two of the princess's bobby pins from the crystal tray by the mirror, then flew to the door. Once there, they examined the keyhole, then using the bobby pins they began to pick the lock. They had only been at it a moment when someone banged hard on the other side of the door and aggressively pushed down the door handle, knocking the lock-picking fairies out of the way.

"YOUR HIGHNESS?" bellowed a voice beyond the door. It was Captain Simperington. "ARE YOU ALL RIGHT?"

"Simpers?" cried the princess, leaping to the door. She had never been so happy to hear anyone in her whole life. "Simpers, can you get us out?"

"The door appears to be locked, Your Highness."

"Yes, we know that, Simpers," she said. "Merrie locked us in here, and she's taken the key."

"I'll run down and get the master key," said the captain.

"NO, there isn't time. She's going to hurt the unicorn."

"Right. I'll have to break the door down, miss. Stand well back, please."

Eleanor scooped Joyce off the table, shouted, "Take cover!" to the palace fairies, and dashed to the far side of the bed. She and Joyce fixed their eyes on the door.

The palace fairies scurried behind the crystal jar and huddled together, knees shaking. Mr. Yeats did not huddle, nor had he scurried, but had anyone been paying close attention they would have noticed that his customary glide had been a tad speedier than usual.

BAM! The first time Simpers hit the door, it bounced in its frame.

BAM! The second time, wood splintered away from the doorjamb, the lock broke free, and Simpers came flying into the room. As he landed on the carpet, the two fairies were catapulted off his shoulders. They rolled commando-style as they landed, then once upright they leapt into the air and sped back to their posts.

Princess Eleanor ran and hugged her bodyguard.

"Thank you, Simpers," she said, helping him up.

"Your Highness," he said with a bow. "I came as soon as I could. Are you all right?"

"I am now, thank you," she replied, heading toward the door. "Let's go. We don't have much time. Joyce?" Joyce flew to her shoulder.

"Your Highness?" called Mr. Yeats. Princess Eleanor stopped and turned. "What can we do to help?" he asked.

Princess Eleanor paused, then said with authority, "We'll need everyone on standby. The captain and I will assess the situation, then let you know what we need you to do." She glanced at her bodyguard and saw him look from her to Mr. Yeats and back again.

"By the way, Simps, this is Joyce," said Eleanor, with a sideways nod to Joyce on her shoulder.

Joyce waved to the captain. He bowed to her, then winced.

The princess laughed. "Ha! Caught you!" she said as she ran out the door and down the corridor. "Joyce said you could see fairies, too," she called over her shoulder. "Why didn't you tell me?"

"Not really the sort of thing one puts on one's job application, Your Highness," replied the captain as he trotted beside her. "Might look a bit odd."

"I suppose it would," agreed Eleanor. "But aren't you going to introduce me to your friends?"

"Ahem, this is Cedric Fellowes on my left," answered Simpers. Cedric bowed. "And this is Anatole Robertson," Simpers added, pointing to his right shoulder. Anatole bowed as well. "They're secret service."

"Ooh!" said Eleanor, nodding shyly at the two rather formal and stiff-looking fairies. Then she smiled and gave them a wave and the pair of them blushed slightly and waved back.

They looked so goofy when they did this that Joyce wondered how she'd ever thought them scary.

Back in the princess's bedroom the palace fairies stood on the dressing table and stared at the broken door.

"How zose big people do rush and crash about," said Madame Lardon.

"Ah, but with good reason," added Mr. Yeats. "Come along, madame. You heard Her Highness. We must put the entire staff on standby. Let's go."

Then they spread their elegant wings and, with the fairy footmen following at a respectable distance, flew swiftly back to the door in the cornice.

Chapter 21

An Exceptional Discovery

As they rushed through the palace, the princess told Simpers everything they'd discovered. The captain had one or two revelations of his own. He told her that Cedric and Anatole, who had been watching Merrie for some time, were certain she was the one selling stories to the papers, but they did not have enough evidence to prove it. Simpers also told her how more than once he had seen the governess telling the king and queen that Eleanor was already asleep when they had come to read her a bedtime story. This information made Eleanor's cheeks flush an angry red, but she swallowed her fury and kept calm.

They crossed the great entrance hall and were just about to go through the main door when Captain Simperington stopped.

"We'd better not go that way, Your Highness," he said.

The princess and Joyce looked through the glass door. In the far corner of the courtyard a large group of people were gathered around a little platform.

"Who are they?" asked Joyce.

"The paparazzi!" exclaimed Princess Eleanor.

"Press photographers," explained Simpers. "And journalists."

"Look! Television people, too," cried Eleanor. She was right. Several television camera crews were setting up their equipment.

"Merrie!" Eleanor cried. "She's going to show the unicorn to the world."

"It certainly looks that way, Your Highness," said Simpers, setting off toward the servants' stairs. "This way, miss." With Joyce still on her shoulder, Eleanor hurried through the door that the captain was holding open.

In the far corner of the courtyard heated words were being exchanged between some of the so-called gentlemen and ladies of the press.

"Look here," said Nigel Rees-Luff of the *Times*, puffing out his narrow pigeon chest. "I was promised an exclusive, so why don't all you tabloid types buzz orf!"

"Watch it, you big toff," replied Arthur Glibson of the *Scrounge*. "I paid for an h'exclusive too, you know, and . . . 'ere—well, 'ow many h'exclusives can you 'ave?"

"Well, certainly no more than five or six," replied Rees-Luff. "Any more, and it's just not on."

Terry White of the *Scar* rolled his eyes and tutted. "What is that woman up to this time?" he grumbled to his neighbor.

Dexter Philbrick of the *Stun* was not amused. "She's h'obviously playing us all for mugs, if you ask me. Selling us all h'exclusives, then pocketing the dosh. If she keeps misbehaving like this, I might have to be doing a bit of an h'exclusive 'palace mole exposure.' 'Ere, something's happening over there."

On the platform the builders had just hung a large banner. On it was the J.J.R. logo and the words:

ANNOUNCING
~~ AN ~~
EXCEPTIONAL DISCOVERY

And below that, in smaller type:

And below that, in even smaller type:

When they saw the banner, the journalists stopped gossiping and started scribbling, and the photographers started clicking their cameras as though this was the most important story of the century.

Beyond the door to the servants' quarters, Captain Simperington quickly led the princess and Joyce down a flight of stairs, then through the warren of offices, garages, and storerooms that lay beneath the palace.

Joyce was beginning to get worried. The captain seemed to know where he was going, but the route he was taking was anything but direct. There seemed to be no end to the maze through which he was leading them. She was just about to lose faith when the captain ran up a flight of rough stone steps at the end of a garage.

"No one uses this entrance at the back of the stables anymore," he said as he opened the door at the top. It creaked on its hinges. "But it suits our needs very well today."

"Simpers, you're the best," exclaimed the princess as the sweet smell of hay and horses rushed out to greet them.

"Thank you, Your Highness," said Captain Simperington humbly. "Now, this way please."

Just as the princess and her group were entering the stables by its back door, Merrie was leading the three Americans out of the front one.

The men from the institute were excited. Their faces were flushed and their eyes were gleaming. Two were discussing tests they'd like to perform on the "specimen," while the third, Professor Wursteinmunster, was bawling into his phone. "Ya gotta see this, sir," he yelled. "Uh-huh. Yup, as soon as you can."

When the professor had finished his call, he looked and noticed for the first time the crowd of journalists around the platform in the corner. He stopped in his tracks when he saw the banner.

"What the heck is this, Merrieweather?" he said.

"You've called a press conference? I thought you promised absolute secrecy!" hissed the professor.

"I don't believe I ever used those exact words, Cregg," replied Merrie. "Don't forget that I've agreed to let J.J. buy the beast, so *you* will be getting the unicorn to take home with you. What's the harm in announcing your good fortune—not to mention your team's dedication to the search for mythical beasts, etc., etc.—to the world's press?"

The professor narrowed his eyes and was about to say something when the institute's Sikorsky S-76C++ helicopter landed smack in the middle of the palace courtyard.

Merrie left him and tottered off toward the billionaire, who had emerged from the helicopter wearing a loud Hawaiian shirt, Bermuda shorts, and a blue baseball cap with the institute's logo on the front. He held on to his hat as the helicopter took off behind him.

The only thing remotely attractive about J. J. Rosenthal was his money. He had mottled, papery skin and a bulbous nose like an old strawberry. He smiled as he shook Merrie's hand, but his pale blue eyes remained frosty.

"Mr. Rosenthal, J.J., it is an honor, sir," enthused Merrie. "If you'll please come this way. I'll be bringing out the unicorn presently, but first I've arranged for your Professor Wursteinmunster to say a few words."

"A speech?" snorted the billionaire. "Are you telling me that—" Merrie cut him off.

"You don't mind, do you? It was Professor Wursteinmunster's idea," she lied as she rushed the man through the crowd and pushed him into a seat that had been reserved for him in the front row.

On the platform, Professor Wursteinmunster stepped up to the podium and tapped a couple of the microphones.

"Are these things on?" he asked. Feedback squealed through the courtyard. "I guess that's a yes," he said, laughing nervously. No one laughed with him.

Joyce barely recognized the unicorn when she saw him. He looked terrible. His once-snowy white coat was dark gray and had started to fall out in large patches. His horn and hooves were completely mottled with dark spots, and the gold of his mane and tail no longer sparkled. His beautiful bright eyes were pitifully dull. Tears spilled down Joyce's cheeks. She left Eleanor's shoulder and flew across the stall to him.

"I'm sorry," she whispered as she stroked his

velvety muzzle. "I'm so, so sorry." The unicorn whinnied softly. Joyce brushed the tears from her cheeks. "Don't worry," she said. "We'll get you home soon, I promise we—"

She was interrupted by a piercing electronic whine.

"The press conference must be starting," said Simpers as he entered Lemon's stall.

"Did you speak with Hobbs?" asked the princess.

"Yes, Your Highness," the captain assured her. "He'll bring a horse van through the back entrance for us."

"Good. Now let's think about this carefully." Eleanor was quiet for a moment, a steely, determined look on her face.

Joyce was amazed how grown-up the princess seemed now. She glanced over at Simpers and saw that he was watching the princess with a look of wonder.

"Here's the situation," announced Eleanor. "Pretty soon Merrie or one of her 'experts' will be coming back for the unicorn so that they can show him to that pack of hyenas out there. With Hobbs's help we can get him away from here before that, but we've got to make sure it's a clean getaway. That's essential. Once Merrie and her experts discover he's gone, they'll be after us. We must buy more time."

"How?" asked Joyce, puzzled.

"We need to create some kind of a diversion," said Simpers.

"A diversion?" said Eleanor. "That's it! But what can we do?"

"Well . . . ," mumbled Joyce, thinking out loud, "if we had another unicorn, we could put that on the stage and that would distract them." Joyce shook her head. "Another unicorn? I must be losing my marbles." She looked up and found the princess and the captain were both staring at her.

"I . . . er—" she began, but Eleanor cut her off.

"Joyce, that's it!" she cried. "Another unicorn? You are brilliant! It might just work, but we're going to need a lot of help. Right! Anatole?" Anatole bowed. "Inform Mr. Yeats of the situation and tell him we need him here ASAP. Cedric? Alert the captain of the fairy guards and have him send me as many troops as he can. Simpers? Fetch bandages, gold paint (non-toxic if possible), cardboard tubes, white flour or talcum powder, glue, and duct tape, and bring as much as you can. Joyce and I will stay here and make sure that neither Merrie nor any of those 'experts' take the unicorn out there. Any questions?"

"Ahem . . . with all due respect, Your Highness,"

said Simpers deferentially, "wouldn't it be better if I stayed here to guard the unicorn?"

"Normally, yes, it would," agreed the princess. "But as I've just seen, you know your way about the palace. I have no idea where to find the things we need, and you do." Captain Simperington hesitated. "Go, Simpers. Joyce and I can handle this."

Simpers gave the princess a piercing look, then nodded. "Yes, Your Highness, I believe you can." He bowed, then set off at a run toward the back door.

Joyce watched him go, a little concerned. "How exactly are you and I supposed to stop anyone from taking the unicorn?" she asked.

Princess Eleanor shrugged. "I have absolutely no idea, Joyce. Let's just hope Simps gets back before anyone tries to."

Chapter 22

THE PRINCESS ELEANOR

At the podium in the corner of the courtyard Professor Cregg Wursteinmunster cleared his throat.

"Ahem. Good afternoon, ladies and gentlemen, my name is Professor Cregg Wursteinmunster, and I'm from the J. J. Rosenthal Institute for the Academic Investigation of the Paranormal. We were invited here today to verify the genuineity of an alleged mythical animal currently residing in the Royal stables.

"My colleagues and I are very much aware that as scientists"—someone in the crowd snorted loudly at this—"we are risking a great deal. As internationally respected men and women of science"—there was

another snort and someone else blew a raspberry—
"our reputations"—three snorts, two raspberries, and a
"ha!"—"OUR livelihoods and indeed our sanity"—
four snorts, three raspberries, another "ha!" and a pro-
nounced "shussssh!" from Merrie—"OUR SANITY
are at stake. We are all aware of that. But I say to you
now, ladies and gentlemen, with my hand on my
heart, that we are willing to put it all, and I do mean
EVERYTHING, on the line and tell you that, having
examined the animal in question, we absolutely and
utterly, without any doubt, believe it to be a genuine
UNICORN!"

That got everyone's attention. Suddenly all the men
and women of the press were out of their seats jeering
derisively and yelling questions at the professor.

At the back of the crowd Merrie smiled, then she
turned and trotted toward the stables.

In Lemon's stall Joyce jumped when she heard the
deafening roar from outside.

"What's that?" asked Joyce, grabbing the princess's shoulder.

The princess looked equally startled. "It's the
press. I'm guessing that someone just told them about
the unicorn. That means they'll be coming to get him
any minute."

The princess suddenly held a finger to her lips. "Shush!" she whispered urgently. "Joyce! Listen!"

Joyce listened. She could hear Merrie's grating voice singing. "Bells will ring, ting a ling a ling . . . that's aMORay!"

With Joyce on her shoulder, the princess crept to the stall's half door and peeped through the sackcloth curtain.

The governess was dancing up the cobbled aisle of the stable using a broom as a dance partner. She set one end of it on the ground, then twirled about it.

"And the moon hits your eye," she crooned. "Like a big pizza pie . . . thaaaat's aMORay!"

The princess shrank back and crouched down behind the stable door.

"Joyce, we can't let her take him," she whispered.

"Then tell her not to," said Joyce. "She'll have to do what you say if you speak to her the way you just spoke to the fairy butler or the captain."

Eleanor blinked at Joyce, then shook her head. "I don't think so, she—"

Suddenly the stall door flew open and bashed right into the princess's knees. Eleanor bit her lip to stop from crying out.

"Now then, my little beauty," cawed Merrie as she pushed through the curtain. She stopped in the doorway and, licking her lips, stared greedily at the unicorn. She cast a nervous eye at Lemon, then, satisfied that the princess's pony seemed docile enough, took a deep breath and set off toward the unicorn. She had a horse blanket draped over one arm, and in her hands she held a thick rope with a loop tied at one end. "Come along, you big bag o' bones," she said with forced confidence as she approached him. "On your feet, that's right. Time to go and meet your soon-to-be new owner."

"New owner?" breathed Eleanor. She and Joyce watched Merrie from behind the stall door, both knowing they ought to do something but unable to think just what that might be.

"Look at Lemon," whispered Joyce.

Eleanor looked and saw Lemon's ears were back. The pony was tossing her head and showing the whites of her eyes. Suddenly she let out a piercing whinny, bolted across the stall, and stopped smack in front of the unicorn, blocking the governess's path.

"Get away, you flea-ridden mule!" Merrie snapped, shaking the rope in Lemon's face. When Lemon didn't move, she swung the rope at her and hit her right on the nose. Both pony and princess reacted instantaneously.

Eleanor leapt to her feet. "Stop that!" she commanded.

Lemon reared up and flailed her heavy hooves in the governess's face.

"Ahahhhahhaha!" wailed Merrie as she fell to the muck-strewn floor.

Eleanor rushed at the downed governess, threw herself on top of her, and pinned her. Merrie struggled, but the princess held firm and didn't let her up.

Merrie stopped struggling and tried another tack.

"Oh, my darling Princess Baby," she said, laughing her twinkly laugh. "What are you doing? Please let me up."

"No," replied the princess, with as much dignity as she could muster while sitting on top of a woman who was lying on a stable floor. "You'll stay here until Captain Simperington returns."

Merrie blinked up at her in surprise.

"Oh, my darling Princess Baby, be reasonable, I was only—"

"I know exactly what you were 'only' doing," retorted the princess.

"I'll take it from here, Your Highness," said Simpers as he rushed into the stall and dropped several cardboard tubes, a few rolls of duct tape, a can of nontoxic gold spray paint, and three large bags of flour on the floor. He picked up the rope Merrie had been holding and hurried to the princess's side. As he helped Eleanor to her feet, Merrie rolled over, and then, with a surprising burst of speed, jumped up and tried to make a break for it. Simpers was too quick for her. He caught her by the arm and yanked her back, then looped the rope around her, pinning her arms to her sides. This done, he picked her up and carried her like a roll of carpet out of the stall.

Merrie was furious. "Let me go!" she squealed. "Let me go this instant, you big ape! You can't do this to me! There are important people out there! Very important people!"

Ignoring her protestations, Simpers tied her to the hitching post. Merrie struggled against the ropes.

"Princess Baby, my darling, my love!" she wailed. The princess approached the governess. Merrie smiled. "Oh, please," she begged sweetly. "Please, my love . . . make him untie me. . . . Please, my princess, please, Princess Baby!"

The young princess drew herself up to her full height and took a deep breath.

"My name," she said in a voice that resonated with regal confidence, "is Princess Eleanor. I am not your 'pet' or your 'sweet' or your 'love,' and I am most certainly not your 'Princess Baby.' I am Princess Eleanor of England, Heir Apparent to the English Throne, and you, Margaret Merrieweather, are, from this moment on, officially unemployed."

Merrie stared at the princess, stunned. She was about to speak when Simpers stuck a fat sugar carrot in her mouth and said, "I think Princess Eleanor has heard enough."

It must be said that Princess Eleanor lost points in the grown-up princess department for snickering and snorting at this.

"I knew you could stand up to her," said Joyce, tapping the princess on the ear. "You were absolutely brilliant, Princess Eleanor."

The princess snorted again. "Thanks," she said. "Joyce, I may be a princess, but please, you don't have to be so formal. You can call me Ellie if you like."

"All right," replied Joyce. "Hey, Ellie?"

"Yes?" said Eleanor.

"You were absolutely brilliant!" laughed Joyce.

Just then the barn doors at the back end of the stable creaked open. Daylight flooded in as a small horse van was speedily backed up along the cobbled aisle. It stopped by Lemon's stall. Hobbs jumped out and ran around to open up the back doors.

"We'll have to be quick, sir," he told the captain.

"That lot out there are demanding to see the unicorn. Could get ugly."

"Very good," replied Simpers. "Proceed."

"Excuse me, Hobbs," said Princess Eleanor, leading the unicorn to the stall door. "Would you please put this poor creature in the horse van?"

"Right-ho, Your Highness." Hobbs touched his finger to his forehead, then, respectfully taking the unicorn's lead rope from the princess, he clacked his tongue twice. "Come along, you poor old duck," he said, carefully leading the sick animal up the ramp into the horse van.

"Thanks. Oh, and Hobbs," added the princess. "As soon as he's settled, come back here. I've got another job for you."

When Princess Eleanor and Joyce returned to the stall they found Anatole, Mr. Yeats, and a large party of house fairies waiting, all anxious to help in any way they could. A moment later Cedric arrived with three squadrons of palace fairy guards.

The princess surveyed the assembled fairies. "We have very little time so please listen carefully," she said as she slipped a bridle over Lemon's head and fastened the buckles. She quickly explained to them what needed to be done.

Chapter 23

An h'Ordinary 'Orse!

It didn't take Hobbs long to settle the unicorn in the horse van.

"Your Highness?" he said, entering Lemon's stall. "You said you had another job for m-m-m-me—" Hobbs stopped abruptly, his eyes nearly popping out of his head in astonishment.

It seemed to him that the princess's pony was being magically transformed. A spray can was floating in midair and turning Lemon's tail gold, white powder was cascading down onto her back, and in the middle of her forehead something, someone, was sticking a gold cardboard tube to her bridle with thin strips of tape. It was, without doubt, the queerest thing Hobbs had ever witnessed.

Realizing the groom couldn't see the multitude of fairies working on Lemon's new look, and understanding that seeing paint cans and cardboard tubes floating in midair might be disconcerting, Princess Eleanor took Hobbs by the arm and steered him back out of the stall.

"Hobbs. HOBBS!" she said firmly. "Pay attention. As soon as Lemon's disguise is finished, I want you to put a blanket over her and lead her out to the courtyard and onto that platform. The press out there are expecting to see the unicorn. They are going to see Lemon instead. Captain Simperington and I are going to drive the unicorn back to Swinley Forest. I need you to look after Lemon and make sure she's all right. Will you do that for me?"

"Yes, Your Highness," replied Hobbs in a faraway voice.

"Good man," said the princess.

At the hitching post, Merrie was busy wriggling and squirming in an attempt to loosen her ropes. Slowly, the knots that bound her were beginning to give, but she froze when Captain Simperington came out of the stall. She watched as he hurried to the front of the horse van and climbed in on the driver's side.

"Wait, Simps, wait for us!" called the princess as she raced out of Lemon's stall. She ran past Merrie and disappeared around the far corner of the horse van.

The ex-governess narrowed her eyes, then chuckled and began to wriggle even more furiously than before.

In the cab of the horse van, Simpers was just about to shift into gear when the passenger door was thrown open and Princess Eleanor, with Joyce perched on her shoulder, jumped in. "We're coming, too!" she declared.

Simpers paused with his hand on the gear lever. "With all due respect, Your Highness," he began, "this promises to be a pretty hairy ride. I could take it from here."

Princess Eleanor lifted her chin. "Yes," she said gravely. "I know you could, Captain Simperington, but Joyce and I have to come. We need to put things right. Besides, Joyce needs a ride home to Swinley Forest."

Simpers raised an eyebrow and allowed himself a minute smile.

"Very well, Your Highness," he said, slipping the car into gear. "Is your safety belt fastened?"

"It is."

"And, Joyce, are you holding on securely?"

"I am."

"Then let's go," he said as he released the brake.

"Wait a minute," cried Joyce, suddenly noticing someone was missing. "What about Cedric and Anatole?"

"They're in the back with the unicorn," replied Simpers. "They wanted to make sure he's all right on the journey."

The captain let out the clutch and drove the horse van through the stable's rear doors. Once outside, he headed for the tradesmen's gate.

At the hitching post Merrie stared at the departing horse van so intently it seemed she was burning every detail of it into her brain. When it had left, Merrie smiled to herself, then resumed her wriggling against the ropes.

Outside in the courtyard Professor Wursteinmunster was doing his best to pacify the press. They were getting rowdy and had even begun to throw crumpled coffee cups and soda cans at him. He was about to take cover behind the lectern when he heard the clip-clop of hooves on the cobbles and saw Hobbs leading a small, blanketed, horse-like animal toward the platform. The unicorn was entirely covered with a blanket. It was draped over his head like a monk's cowl, completely covering the gold horn. Only the faintest hint of a white muzzle could be seen.

The professor rubbed his hands together gleefully, then turned to face his skeptical audience. "Ahem, quiet please, thank you for your patience, ladies and gentlemen. I believe that our very special guest has now arrived."

The crowd fell silent as Hobbs led the blanket-covered Lemon onto the platform. The members of the press, all hardened professionals, surged forward. Some of them even gasped and oohed as they caught a glimpse of a gold hoof beneath the hem of the blanket.

Journalists craned their necks and scribbled, photographers' cameras clicked and whirred, and the TV cameras began to record.

"Ladies and gentlemen," Wursteinmunster announced. "I am indeed most honored to present to you the world's first real, live"—he reached over and, still looking out at the audience, threw Lemon's blanket off with dramatic flair—"UNICORN!"

There was a roar as everyone struggled to get a better look, then suddenly the crowd fell quiet again.

The professor's smile froze. He didn't understand why the journalists looked so bewildered. He turned slowly and when he saw the unicorn he nearly fell off the platform. What the heck! It was a horse! A pony! A pony covered in flour with its hooves painted gold and a gold cardboard horn taped to its head.

"That's an 'orse! An h'ordinary 'orse!" someone snorted.

The press erupted in a loud volley of boos, hisses, whistles, and outraged shouts. "What's the meaning of this?" "Who do you think you are kidding?" "What is this? April Fools' Day in June?" "What will Their Majesties think of this farce?"

Professor Wursteinmunster tried to regain control of the situation.

"Ladies . . . gentlemen . . . please . . . there has been some mistake."

"You're telling us. That's a pony with an 'orn stuck on it."

"This is not the unicorn we saw, there's been a switcheroo, a prank. Please be patient and let me get to the bottom of this."

But the press had lost all patience. The photographers began to pack up their cameras, the reporters put away their recorders and notebooks, and the television crews were about to unplug their equipment, when all of a sudden they heard a chilling scream. A moment later they saw a petite, disheveled woman with copper-colored hair stagger out of the stables, rope trailing behind her.

"That's Miss Merrieweather, the princess's governess!" shouted Arthur Glibson.

"Oh, help!" she wailed pitifully as she rushed up onto the platform and with great drama threw herself into the professor's arms. "Oh, plee-heese . . . ," she sobbed, clinging to the professor somewhat tighter than necessary. "Call the guards . . . the princess . . . Princess Eleanor . . . my darling . . . she's been . . . KIDNAPPED!"

The press went nuts. This was more like it. Here was a real story! Cameras clicked and flashed, and the unicorn fiasco was instantly forgotten as they pushed forward, eager to capture every last detail of this terrible event.

The horse van was just turning onto Brompton Road when Joyce, Eleanor, and Captain Simperington heard the news of the princess's kidnapping on the car radio.

"What?" cried Princess Eleanor. "What kidnapping?" She reached for the volume control and turned up the sound.

Merrie's tearful voice came over the airwaves loud

and clear. "My beautiful princess," she sobbed. "My Princess Eleanor! Ohh hoo-hoo. Why did I let this happen?"

"Oh, that woman!" cried the princess.

"Listen," said Joyce.

The radio announcer went on. "In breaking news from Buckingham Palace it appears that Her Royal Highness Princess Eleanor has been kidnapped by her bodyguard Captain James Simperington, age thirty-three. The princess was visiting her pony in the palace stables accompanied by her devoted governess, Margaret Merrieweather, age thirty-five . . ."

"Thirty-five!" screamed Eleanor and Simpers together.

"Shushhhh," said Joyce.

". . . when it appears the bodyguard brutally attacked Ms. Merrieweather and tied her up before absconding with the princess."

Merrie's quavering voice came on again. "It was awful," she sobbed. "Oh, the monster. He lifted her up like a rag doll and ran to the horse van with her."

"Can you tell us anything about this horse van? Any details?"

"No . . . I . . . er . . . oh, it's all a blur . . . no, wait . . . the license plate number . . . it was . . ." Then in a very clear voice she said, "B-J-H-six-nine-F. Did you get that? B-J-H-six-nine-F. Oh, my poor, poor darling . . . *sniff . . .*"

The news announcer took over. "Countrywide police and armed forces personnel have been put on alert to find that horse van and bring the princess back unharmed. Their Majesties have been informed of this terrible event and it is thought that the Royal Couple is returning immediately from their state visit to Denmark. They are expected to arrive back in the country within the hour. Her Majesty the queen is said to be in a state of shock. The palace has just released a statement decreeing that Captain Simperington, previously a loyal and trusted servant, will be dealt with fairly, if he gives himself up and returns the princess unharmed within the next hour. "

In the horse van Simpers turned to the princess. "Your Highness," he said, "the whole country will be looking for us. The police, the army, the air force, they'll be coming after us in helicopters and high-speed vehicles—"

"What are our chances of outrunning them, Simps?" asked the princess.

"In a horse van?" Simpers took a big breath, then blew it out. "Not great, Your Highness. But I do have impeccable driving skills, and I'm willing to give it a try."

"Oh, Simpers, you are brilliant!" cried Princess Eleanor. "Get us to Swinley as fast as you can."

"Very good, Your Highness. Joyce, settle somewhere secure, and both of you hold tight."

Simpers spun the steering wheel to the left, deftly pulled in front of a red double-decker bus, and gunned it down the bus lane. At sixty miles an hour the horse van bounced about mercilessly. Princess Eleanor clung to the handle above her window as the cab swayed from side to side. Joyce clung to Eleanor's collar.

"I hope the unicorn's all right back there," shouted Joyce above the noisy din of the engine.

"Cedric and Anatole will be doing their best to keep him calm," Simpers assured her. "I just hope they're not singing to him."

In the back of the horse van the poor unicorn was laying on his side with his eyes closed, while Cedric and Anatole rocked comfortably in the crook of his velvety neck and sang improvised harmonies of their favorite country and western songs.

Captain Simperington was a skilled and daring driver, and they were through Earls Court in minutes. They would soon be on the motorway. From there it was a straight run to Swinley. As long as they didn't hit traffic, they might, just might, make it to the forest before they were caught. They flew along the fast lane of the Great West Road and were making good time, but just as they joined the motorway, they were greeted by the unwelcome sight of red brake lights lighting up. It didn't faze Simpers. He cut across three lanes and sped up the hard shoulder.

"Listen!" said the princess. They all heard the distant sirens. They seemed to be coming from every direction. Above them they could see a number of police and army helicopters in the city skies.

"They're going to catch us before we're even out of the city," groaned the princess.

"No, they won't," said Simpers. He put his left hand to his ear and spoke into the microphone in his cuff. "Anatole, Cedric, do you copy?" he said. "Listen up. Effective immediately. Contact the heads of the fairy forces. Tell them to enact emergency measures code A-seven-three-six-six case specific, repeat code A-seven-three-six-six case specific. The pylon pixies can set up scrambler stations all over the southlands. That should block all communications. Yes? Fine. Let me know. Over."

"Simps?" shouted the princess above the rattle of the engine. "Isn't that dangerous? I mean, no radio communications? What about planes? Ambulances?"

"Don't worry, Your Highness," replied Simpers.

"The pylon pixies have the technology to scramble only the radio communications that pertain to us. It'll make it more difficult for them to track us."

"I had no idea that fairies were so well organized," laughed the princess.

"Neither had I!" cried Joyce.

"Hold tight, please!" shouted Simpers as he swung out into the now moving traffic to avoid a hedgehog on the hard shoulder.

Chapter 24

THE FOREST

On the platform in the palace courtyard Merrie was still digging her nails into the professor's arm.

"Psst," she said out of the corner of her mouth to Wursteinmunster. "This isn't over yet. I know where they're headed."

"Where?" muttered Wursteinmunster.

"I'll show you," whispered Merrie. "Is your helicopter close by?"

"Sure, the pilot will have parked it on the Royal helipad."

"*Parked?*" She rolled her eyes and let go of his arm. "You don't *park* a helicopter!" she sneered. The professor opened his mouth, but Merrie didn't give him a chance to speak. "Never mind!" she snapped. "Gather up your people and meet me at the helipad in five, and tell your crazy boss to bring his checkbook. You'll get your unicorn, no sweat."

The drive to Swinley Castle usually takes just over an hour if the traffic is light and drivers are staying within the speed limit. On this occasion the traffic was heavy, but with Simpers driving like a maniac, they made it to the castle in less than half that time.

As Simpers pulled up to the castle gate, he wound down the window and showed the armed guard his pass.

The guard was very young, and he looked nervous. His Adam's apple bobbed up and down at his throat.

"If you wouldn't mind stepping out, please, sir," he said curtly.

Simpers clenched his jaw. "I do mind, actually. I am here on very important business."

"If you would just step out of the vehicle, sir." The guard lowered his rifle to show he meant business.

Princess Eleanor leaned across to the driver's-side window. "Excuse me," she said, "do you know who I am?"

The guard looked shocked to see her, then recovered his composure and bowed. "Yes, indeed I do, Your Highness."

"Then let us in, please."

"Sorry, Your Highness, can't do that. We are on red alert. There was a telephone call from the palace forty minutes ago saying that if this man showed up we was to place him under arrest, and that is what I am trying to do. Now, sir, if you will kindly step out of the car."

"Do you know why you're supposed to arrest him?" asked Princess Eleanor in a very patient voice.

"He has h'apparently kidnapped you, Your Highness," replied the guard.

"Well, he hasn't. I'm here, aren't I? Safe and sound. Now, let us through."

"Sorry, miss, can't do that, miss, can't disobey a direct order, miss. Now, sir, if you'll just step out of the car."

"Oh, for heaven's sakes!" groaned the princess as she flumped back in her seat. Joyce tapped her on the ear.

"Ellie," she said. "I've got an idea. Keep Simpers in the car. Tell him not to get out. I'll be back soon."

"Be careful," said the princess as Joyce flew out of the window.

Joyce shot past the human guard unseen and flew through the open door of the gatehouse. Once inside, she saw a large panel of electronic switches and soon saw the one she needed. It was a large orange button, conveniently labeled "gate." Joyce landed beside it and was about to press it when she felt a hand on her shoulder.

Joyce looked up and found William Butler staring down at her. Behind him stood Daphne, smiling.

"Hello, Joyce," she said. "Mr. Yeats at the palace called to let us know you were on your way. They sounded very impressed with you. Now, Dad's got something to tell you, haven't you, Dad?"

William Butler looked embarrassed. "Yes, well, erm, no time to waste on that now. That gate button's a bit stiff, so, if you'll allow me."

"Dad!" snapped Daphne, stamping her foot. "Say it!"

William Butler's discomfort increased. "All right, Daphne!" he responded testily. "Joyce, you were right and I was wrong and I'm truly sorry I didn't help you in the first place. Now, you get back to the princess while I deal with that button!" Joyce shot toward the door while Mr. Butler, respectable Royal servant and staunch protector of the law, turned around and plunked his ample bottom down on the button. Outside the gate swung open.

Joyce had to fly fast to catch up with the horse van

as it accelerated away from the gate. She only just made it through the window before Simpers put his foot down again and turned sharply onto the lane that led to the meadow.

"Oh!" cried Joyce as the forest came into view. "Oh, look! That's why Daphne's father said I'd been right!"

The forest was dying. The leaves were brown, and even though it was still early in the summer some of the trees were already bare. The forest was beginning to look just like Warning Wood.

"Please hurry," said Joyce, desperate to get the unicorn home as soon as they could.

Simpers shifted gears as the horse van pulled off the lane and onto the uneven terrain of the meadow. He drove straight through the stony brook, then powered up the slope toward the forest. When he was close to the trees, he suddenly shifted gears and grabbed the parking brake lever, spinning the horse van so that it came to a neat stop with its rear pointing conveniently toward the woods.

"Wow, Simps!" said the princess as they got out. "Will you teach me to drive like that?"

"How old are you now?" the captain shouted from his side of the horse van.

"Ten," she replied as they met at the back.

Simpers slipped the bolt, opened the doors, and lowered the ramp.

"Maybe next year then," he said with a grin. "All right?"

"Wonderful!" The princess beamed.

Inside the horse van, Anatole and Cedric hovered beside the unicorn. Cedric looked a little green around the gills.

"Remind me never to ride in the back of one of these things again, Tolly," he groaned.

"Don't be such a wuss, Ced," Anatole chided. "You'll be fine in a minute. Now help me get him out of here."

They flew to the unicorn's head and gently whispered in his ear.

"Time to open your eyes," said Cedric.

"Look where you are," added Anatole.

"You're home," they both said together. "Look, it's your forest."

The unicorn opened his eyes and lifted his head. He seemed to perk up when he saw the trees, and a faint spark returned to his eye. Princess Eleanor entered the back of the horse van and encouraged him to get up. She led him down the ramp. Joyce hovered and hung back with Cedric and Anatole. All three of them sensed this was a private moment.

The princess and the unicorn stood at the edge of the forest. She hugged his neck and buried her face in his mane to hide her tears.

"I'm sorry," she sniffed. "I never meant for you to get hurt." The unicorn whinnied softly, then rested his head over her shoulder. They stood like that at the edge of the trees for a long time.

Joyce, Anatole, Cedric, and Captain Simperington saw what the princess could not. The unicorn was changing. His coat was turning white, his horn and hooves were gold once again, and the luster was returning to his mane and tail. By the time the princess pulled away from him, he looked proud and strong and as beautiful as he'd been on the day she first saw him.

The princess laughed joyfully when she saw how his beauty and health had returned. "You must go," she said, pointing at the trees. "You aren't safe out here." The unicorn pawed the ground with a shining hoof. The princess shook her head. "No, we can't play now. I'll come and find you another day, I promise." The unicorn nibbled at her pockets. Eleanor patted his neck. "Yes, I'll bring sugar carrots for you." The unicorn stepped back and whinnied louder, then he trotted toward the trees.

"Thank you for letting him go, Ellie," whispered

Joyce as she landed on the princess's shoulder. The princess didn't say anything. She just smiled, though her eyes sparkled with tears.

At the edge of the woods the unicorn spun around, and with a whinny that shook the trees he rose up on his hind legs and pawed at the air, his golden hooves catching fire in the sunlight. Then he dropped down and turned toward the forest.

"I am so glad you're going back where you belong," Princess Eleanor called.

"And I'm so glad you're glad, Princess *Ell-a-nor*," said Merrie as she stepped out from behind a tree. "I'm always glad when you're glad, don't you know that?"

"Run!" cried the princess. "Unicorn! RUN!" But it was too late. A large net spun out from the dark of the woods and landed over him. He bucked and whinnied and fought but it was no good. The unicorn was caught and he couldn't get away.

Chapter 25

Twenty-one Million Dollars!

The men from the J. J. Rosenthal Institute ran out from behind the trees, took hold of the net, and held it down to make sure that the unicorn could not escape.

J. J. Rosenthal walked out of the woods. As he approached the unicorn, a change came over him. Up until that moment the billionaire's face had resembled nothing so much as a tightly closed fist, but now he looked like he must have as a little boy. His blue eyes were open wide and his face was full of wonder.

He knelt down and very, very carefully lifted the net from the animal's head and disentangled it from the horn. For a moment, Joyce thought all was not lost. Perhaps this strange man would let the unicorn go. Eleanor was thinking the same thing. They were both very wrong.

Without warning, J. J. Rosenthal whipped a red velvet halter from behind his back and slipped it over the unicorn's neck. Then, like a cowboy securing a steer, he deftly tipped the unicorn over and tied his legs together so he couldn't run. J. J. Rosenthal's face was hard as steel again when he stood up, and his cold eyes glinted as he looked at his prize.

He slapped the dust off his hands and pulled a piece of paper from his pocket.

"I believe I have what I came for," he drawled. "I'm mighty grateful to you, Miss Merrieweather. Here's your check. Twenty-one million was the agreed-upon price, wasn't it?"

Merrie nodded enthusiastically as the billionaire handed her the check. She eyed the amount, kissed the check, and put it in her pocket. She pulled her cell phone out and started to text. Simpers seized the moment and moved toward the unicorn. But Merrie couldn't allow that. Without taking her eyes from her phone, she pulled a pearl-handled pistol from her pocket and pointed it at him.

"I don't think so, Captain," she said as she finished her text message with one thumb.

Joyce flew to the governess's head and started to pull at her coppery hair. Merrie twitched and jerked her head about, but managed to keep the gun pointing at the captain.

"Hold on, Joyce," yelled Anatole as he and Cedric flew by. She watched them shoot into the air. When they were little more than specs in the sky, they turned and zoomed down toward Merrie. They hit her on the inside of her wrist with such force that the gun flew out of her hand.

Simpers dropped to the ground and rolled commando-style to where the gun lay. He picked it up and, as he rolled upright, balanced the muzzle on his forearm, training it on Merrie.

"Get behind me, please, Your Highness," he instructed the princess. Eleanor did so.

Now Simpers turned and pointed the gun at the billionaire. "Let the unicorn go," he said very slowly. "No sudden movements, please."

The flinty-eyed billionaire crouched down and untied the velvet rope. The unicorn staggered to its feet. "And get that collar off him," said the captain in a dangerous voice. "Ready, Joyce?" he called.

J. J. Rosenthal's head jerked up and he glared furiously at the captain, hate brimming in his eyes. "How did you know my name was Joyce?" he growled.

The captain ignored him. He was watching Joyce, the fairy, who was clinging to the unicorn's mane and leaning close to his ear.

"It's all right," she said in a soothing voice. "Once that horrid collar's off, you can go. Steady, steady, now run!" cried Joyce as the velvet loop fell to the ground.

Joyce clung to the unicorn's mane as he reared up again. He flailed his golden hooves in the billionaire's terrified face, then he dropped down, tore into the trees, and was gone.

In the very center of the forest, in the middle of the fairy town of Swinley Hope, Sam Swain stood alone in the empty market square. He was the first to notice the change in the breeze. He stopped sweeping, looked up at the treetops, and smiled.

"Well done, Joyce," he murmured to himself. "Well done."

Now dozens of police cars and army jeeps raced across the meadow and up the hill.

"Help! Help! Help!" cried Merrie, pointing at Simpers. "Over here. This is the man you want. He's the kidnapper. He's got a gun! He's going to shoot the princess!"

The first jeep stopped and five guards leapt out

with their assault rifles at the ready. They ran past the princess and the captain, then encircled Merrie and trained their guns on her.

"What are you doing?" she demanded.

"No sudden movements now, miss," said one of the guards.

"What's going on?" Eleanor whispered to Simpers.

"I'm not sure, Your Highness, but I think it's going to be good."

Just then Princess Eleanor noticed J. J. Rosenthal, Professor Wursteinmunster, and the two other men heading into the forest.

"Of all the cheek," she said. She marched over and tapped J.J. sharply on the shoulder.

"You do realize," she said authoritatively, "that you are trespassing on the grounds of a Royal estate."

The Americans laughed in her face. Princess Eleanor gave them a look that stopped them in mid-laugh.

"What's it to you, shorty?" sneered J. J. Rosenthal, who had dealt with tougher customers than her in his time.

"Not much," replied Princess Eleanor, "but I think it's only fair to warn you that there are only two crimes for which one can still be hung in this country, and you are all committing one of them right now. We still have some gallows in the castle yard, if you're interested."

The Americans looked first at each other, then back at her. Princess Eleanor smiled sweetly, then turned and walked back to where Simpers waited. "Didn't your father abolish the death penalty entirely, miss?" murmured Simpers.

"He did, Simps, but I don't think they know that. Look at them run." The princess and her bodyguard couldn't help but snicker.

"That check's already canceled, Merrieweather!" yelled J. J. Rosenthal as he and the others ran like rats to where their helicopter was hidden.

"NOOOOOOOOOOO!" screamed Merrie. "You can't do that to me!" She stopped and squinted at a short, squat man who had just jumped out of one of the army jeeps and was hurrying toward her.

"Dexter Philbrick!" she gasped in astonishment.

"Well, well, look at you, Maggs," he said, opening his notepad and licking the tip of his pencil. "How's about you start earnin' all that money wot you owe my paper by giving us a real h'exclusive on what it's like to be h'exposed as a palace mole, eh? Course, you'll have to dictate it to me from prison, because that's where you'll be for a very long time. The worm 'as turned, my dear, the worm 'as turned. You should have given me that unicorn exclusive. You don't cross the likes of Dexter Philbrick and get away wiv it."

"Take her away," said Captain Simperington.

The guards led Merrie to a jeep. To her dismay, Dexter got in beside her and began to badger her with questions.

The princess forgot all about Merrie as the Royal helicopter appeared over the horizon and flew in low over the meadow. The police and the troops stood to attention as the helicopter landed and its blades began to slow. Princess Eleanor waited beside Simpers and held very still. She hardly breathed as she watched the door open.

Their Highnesses the king and queen rushed out and ran across the grass toward Princess Eleanor. They didn't look all that royal or regal or distant now, and they certainly weren't too busy. They just looked like two parents who had had a nasty shock.

"Oh, Ellie!" cried the queen as she scooped the princess up in her arms and held her close. Eleanor closed her eyes and hugged her mother back as hard as she could. Then she hugged her daddy. She didn't want to cry, but she couldn't help it. She was just so happy to see them.

Eleanor's were not the only tears on the meadow

that afternoon. Most of the big strapping guards, it seemed, had got a bit of something in their eyes.

"Must be the dust kicked up by the helicopter," remarked one. "It's making my eyes water something wicked."

"Must be that," sniffed Captain Simperington as he watched Princess Eleanor and her parents holding hands as they walked back across the meadow toward the castle. "I can't imagine what else it could be."

Chapter 26

COMING HOME

It was market day in Swinley Hope. An autumn market. Carts laden with elderberries and rowan were wheeling into the clearing. Whole chestnuts were being roasted on spits over open fires, and at one stall fairies were pressing fresh juice from great slices of apple. Elsewhere, whole apples were being offered to those who wanted to make jack-o'-lanterns for the coming festival.

High above the market square, a young fairy by the name of Joyce lay on her belly along a twig at the top of her home tree.

"Autumn," she said to herself with a smile, "is

absolutely my favorite season." And she really meant it. Then she remembered that every season was her favorite season and she laughed, causing the twig to bounce beneath her weight.

The summer was over, but that was all right. It had been a long summer that began with her adventures beyond the forest and officially ended today with the first day of school. Joyce gazed down at the pretty scene below, thankful that everything in the forest had recovered as it should have.

She shuddered when she remembered first coming back into the woods with the unicorn. The dreadful smell of rotting vegetation had been everywhere, and the trees had been covered in dead leaves. But as he'd moved deeper into the forest, the trees had regained their color, leaves sprouted, ferns unfurled, and buds began to blossom.

When he had run far into the forest, the unicorn had stopped by the edge of the brook. Joyce had let go of his mane and flown above him. "Goodbye," she'd said. The unicorn had tossed his head twice, turned about, then jumped the brook and bolted into the deepest part of the forest. Joyce had watched him run until she could see him no more. Then she'd flown to Swinley Hope to tell everyone that the unicorn was back.

But everyone had seen the changes in the forest and they already knew the unicorn had returned. The whole of Swinley Hope was celebrating. Joyce's parents and sisters had been overjoyed to see her. "I was terribly worried when you disappeared," Joyce's mother told her, "but then Alderman Choosy himself came to see us. He said the alders had sent you to find the unicorn because you were the only person who could do it. And now you've done it. You've brought him back. Well done, my darling! Oh, well done!"

Her first evening back had been like no other. There'd been a party in the market square and everyone had been there. The whole town had been happy to see her safely back. There'd been many tears and much hugging. Even Alderman Choosy had shaken her hand and congratulated her on a job well done.

Her teacher, Miss Crisp, had been thrilled to see her. She'd hugged Joyce tight and had told her not to worry about the end-of-term exams or anything. Miss Crisp had given her full marks for rescuing the unicorn and bringing him home.

Everyone wanted to hear the story of how the unicorn had been rescued. But when Joyce tried to tell them more about the outside world, she began to see why Sam never talked about his travels. The fairies in Swinley Hope weren't really very interested in anything beyond the forest. They were happy with what they had—their unicorn was back, the forest would soon recover, and they were at an excellent party. What else really mattered?

The party had lasted three whole days and nights. It had been loud, raucous, and fun. Even the alders had danced.

On the first night, Sam had sat and watched the dancing with her.

"I've got some good news for you," he'd said.

"What is it?" Joyce asked.

Sam nodded at the dancers and Joyce saw that one or two had extended their wings and were lifting off the floor as they whirled.

"Flying is acceptable again," he laughed. "You can now be respectable *and* fly in Swinley Hope!"

Sam then told her how, on the night the unicorn had left and the alarms had sounded, the respectable fairies of Swinley Hope had seen the light. Flying, they'd realized as they struggled to get the whole town hidden and packed away, flying was essential to a fairy's survival. It was a very important, perhaps the most important, skill to have.

Now, from her branch, Joyce watched the fairies flit about the market. It was a wonderful sight. Even those fairies whose wings were still too weak were trying hard, and their flying skills would improve with practice.

Gone were the folded, bound, and prettified wings. Soft and supple was no longer desirable. Strong and muscular was the rage. Wing strength and span were valued. Joyce was very happy about that. It was such a relief to be able to fly wherever, whenever she liked. She stretched out her long, lean wings. She had to admit she was rather proud of them.

"Joyce, are you going to school today or not?" asked her mother, who had popped up from the kitchen and now hovered in front of Joyce with her hands on her hips and her wings beating steadily behind her. Her mother's sudden appearance startled Joyce. She wondered, not for the first time, if she'd ever get used to seeing her mother fly.

And did the princess and Joyce ever meet up again? They did. As often as they could. Whenever the princess was staying at the castle, she would spend her afternoons by the edge of the forest and wait for Joyce to meet her. They would go together into the forest to see the unicorn and take him the sugar carrots the princess had promised him. Afterward Joyce and the princess would walk out of the forest and sit on the hill, talking about the times they'd had or about the things they'd like to do when they grew up. They would talk until Captain Simperington came up the hill. Often he would stay and chat with them. And Cedric and Anatole would tell Joyce long and complicated stories about what they'd been up to since they'd seen her last.

But eventually Simpers would look at his watch and tell Her Highness it was time to go. Then he would escort the princess back to the castle for supper, which was now a meal that she shared with her parents every single night of the week.

ACKNOWLEDGMENTS

With thanks to the wonderful Jenny for all her help, the glamorous Gwen for all the glue, and the fabulous Karen and Steve for taking care of F&S and giving me a place to write. Many thanks also to the ever-tolerant Neil, the beautiful Emma, and the undeniably good-looking Christopher for all their patience, faith, and support. And special thanks to the eagle-eyed Jim for his tough-love edit and his belief in this book, and also to the lovely Lisa, who got me back into writing about fairies.

CAROL HUGHES grew up in England, in a seaside town where her parents kept a small hotel. When she got older, she went to art school to study painting. But instead of drawings, she filled her sketchbooks with notes and stories. Not long afterward, she moved to the United States and began writing. She now lives in Los Angeles with her husband and two daughters.

To learn more about Carol,
visit her Web site at carolhughes.us.com.

12/09